Hi, I'm JIMMY!

Like me, you probably noticed the world is run by adults.
But ask yourself: Who would do the best job
of making books that *kids* will love?
Yeah. **Kids!**

So that's how the idea of JIMMY books came to life.
We want every JIMMY book to be so good that when you're finished,
you'll say,

"PLEASE GIVE ME ANOTHER BOOK!"

Give this one a try and see if you agree.
(If not, you're probably an adult!)

JIMMY PATTERSON BOOKS FOR YOUNG READERS

James Patterson Presents
Sci-Fi Junior High by John Martin and Scott Seegert
How to Be a Supervillain by Michael Fry

The Middle School Series by James Patterson
Middle School: The Worst Years of My Life
Middle School: Get Me Out of Here!
Middle School: Big Fat Liar
Middle School: How I Survived Bullies, Broccoli, and Snake Hill
Middle School: Ultimate Showdown
Middle School: Save Rafe!
Middle School: Just My Rotten Luck
Middle School: Dog's Best Friend
Middle School: Escape to Australia

The I Funny Series by James Patterson
I Funny
I Even Funnier
I Totally Funniest
I Funny TV
I Funny: School of Laughs

The Treasure Hunters Series by James Patterson
Treasure Hunters
Treasure Hunters: Danger Down the Nile
Treasure Hunters: Secret of the Forbidden City
Treasure Hunters: Peril at the Top of the World

For exclusives, trailers, and other information, visit jimmypatterson.org.

MIDDLE SCHOOL
ESCAPE TO AUSTRALIA

JAMES PATTERSON
with MARTIN CHATTERTON

Illustrated by Daniel Griffo

JIMMY PATTERSON BOOKS
LITTLE, BROWN AND COMPANY
NEW YORK · BOSTON · LONDON

JIMMY Patterson Books / Little, Brown and Company
Hachette Book Group
1290 Avenue of the Americas, New York, NY 10104
JimmyPatterson.org

First Edition: March 2017

JIMMY Patterson Books is an imprint of Little, Brown and Company, a division of Hachette Book Group, Inc. The Little, Brown name and logo are trademarks of Hachette Book Group, Inc. The JIMMY Patterson name and logo are trademarks of JBP Business, LLC.

Middle School® is a trademark of JBP Business, LLC.

The publisher is not responsible for websites (or their content) that are not owned by the publisher.

The Hachette Speakers Bureau provides a wide range of authors for speaking events. To find out more, go to hachettespeakersbureau.com or call (866) 376-6591.

Library of Congress Cataloging-in-Publication Data
Patterson, James, author. | Chatterton, Martin, author. |
Griffo, Daniel, illustrator.
Title: Escape to Australia / James Patterson ; with Martin Chatterton ; illustrated by Daniel Griffo.
Description: First edition. | New York ; Boston : JIMMY Patterson Books,
Little, Brown and Company, 2017. | Series: Middle school ; book 9 | Summary: The trip to Australia Rafe has won starts badly, but after connecting with a group of misfits he finds a way to do what he does best—create mayhem.
Identifiers: LCCN 2016030382 | ISBN 978-0-316-27262-9 (hc) / 978-0-316-47017-9 (Scholastic ed) / 978-0-316-44047-9 (int'l ed)
Subjects: | CYAC: Middle schools—Fiction. | Schools—Fiction. | Friendship—Fiction. | Americans—Australia—Fiction. | Australia—Fiction. | Humorous stories. | BISAC: JUVENILE FICTION / Humorous Stories. | JUVENILE FICTION / People & Places / Australia & Oceania. | JUVENILE FICTION / Social Issues / Adolescence. | JUVENILE FICTION / Social Issues / New Experience. | JUVENILE FICTION / Family / Alternative Family.
Classification: LCC PZ7.P27653 Esc 2017 | DDC [Fic]—dc23 LC record available at https://lccn.loc.gov/2016030382

10 9 8 7 6 5 4 3 2 1

LSC-C

Printed in the United States of America

TO MORTIMER
AND AGNETHA DeVere,
THe ULTIMATE MIDDLE SCHOOL
SURVIVORS
—M.C.

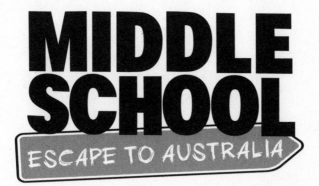

CHAPTER 1

ZOMBiE INVASiON!

You know that icky feeling you get in the pit of your stomach when you look out of your bedroom window at night and see a mob of bloodthirsty Australian zombies heading right at you?

No?

Well, I'm here to tell you that seeing a whole bunch of the walking dead making a beeline for yours truly was definitely NOT one of my better moments. And for any of you who've been keeping up with all things Khatchadorian, you'll know that there has been a *ton* of weirdness in my recent history.

From the look on their dirt-streaked, bug-eyed

faces and the nasty collection of weapons they were waving around—pitchforks, tennis rackets, flaming torches, barbecue tongs, a rusty exhaust pipe from a 2006 Camry—these dudes were serious about claiming the top spot in Rafe Khatchadorian's All-Time Disasters List.

I don't mind admitting I was a teeny-tiny bit FREAKED OUT.

The zombie dudes had made a real effort, too. Do you have any idea how *hard* it would be to find a pitchfork these days? The fact that this mob had come up with THREE of them showed a real level of zombie determination.

Despite the pitchforks, there was, however, one tiny ray of hope that I could cling to: maybe it wasn't *me* they were after. It could be that the zombies had other delicious victims in mind besides the untasty and downright bony Rafe Khatchadorian of Hills Village.

That hope faded quickly when they started chanting: "WE WANT RAFE! WE WANT RAFE!"

I guess that settled it. The seriously messed-up truth was that these guys wanted BLOOD—and lots of it. Very specifically, they wanted *my* blood, which was a real problem. I *like* my blood. Call me selfish, but I want to keep as much of my blood as I possibly can, for as long as I can.

In a weird way, though, a small part of me was kind of proud. It takes a lot to make that many Australian zombies mad, but I, Rafe Khatchadorian, had managed it in just a few short weeks. Ta-da!

Three weeks ago I didn't know a single person in Australia, let alone a zombie, and now I had a baying mob of the undead at the front door. Not bad when you think of it that way.

I'm Rafe, by the way. On a good day—like, a *really* good day—I look like this:

But usually it's more like this:

Okay, I know what you're
probably thinking about
all this zombie stuff:
that it sounds
super exciting and
majorly awesome,
but why should we
listen to a single word you say?

Says you.

Ursula
Le Bon,
book
critic

Yeah, who do you think
you are, Khatchadorian?

I'm so angry
I could crush
a grape!

He's talking
garbage!

MIDDLE
SCHOOL

MIDDLE
SCHOOL

MIDDLE
SCHOOL

Which is totally valid. But to explain everything, we'll have to go back, back through the mists of time, back to the very beginning of the story of how I ended up in this predicament.

Yep, we're going to middle school.

CHAPTER 2

THE GREAT HERNANDEZ MUSTACHE THEORY

We'll get to the zombies later because the BIG news to start off with isn't mutant brain-eaters, it's that (drumroll, please!) I, Rafe Khatchadorian, have managed to stay enrolled at Hills Village Middle School for more than a minute.

That's right, you heard me. Since we last spoke, I have NOT been expelled. Not even suspended! Detention, well…let's not go that far. I'm not perfect.

But for me, not getting kicked out of school is *seriously* awesome, bordering on miraculous and hunkering down right next door to flat-out impossible.

For example, it seems like only yesterday that the seriously scary new vice principal at Hills Village, the knuckle-crunching Charlotte P. Stonecase (a.k.a. the Terror from Room 666, a.k.a. the Skull Keeper), forced me to take part in The Program, a kind of prison camp in the woods for "wayward students."

Wayward is just another way of saying *troublemaking,* and before I could say, "No, wait, I think there's been some kind of mistake," I was shipped off to the Rocky Mountains for a week of *total* attitude realignment.

For a while there it was touch and go, but somehow I survived and made it back from Colorado alive.

Who knows, maybe the bottom line is that VP Stonecase wasn't so far off the mark about what I needed. Maybe she's some sort of cosmic fortune-teller.

Guru Stonecase

Anyway, this whole not-getting-into-major-trouble-at-Hills-Village-Middle-School situation was so *weird* that I was convinced the school had been taken over by pod creatures. You know, the kind of aliens who sneakily make themselves look like the regular people they've eaten until you're the only human left.

Pod Dad

Pod Mom

Pod Kid

I decided to test my theory. The big mistake I made was to test it by pulling Mr. Hernandez's mustache in gym class. You can already see where this is going, right?

Mr. Hernandez was standing in for Mr. Lattimore, our regular gym teacher, and I had some sort of brain-melting idea that pod people might use fake mustaches or something. Looking back on it, I don't know why I thought the aliens could replicate every other single thing about a person except a mustache.

Now, even though he'd just started teaching at Hills Village at the beginning of the year, I'd already learned that Mr. Hernandez was not what

Man! I just can't get this whole mustache thing!

you'd call the forgiving type. In fact, trying to figure out once and for all if Mr. Hernandez was an alien by trying to pull off his mustache would normally have resulted in (at least) a hundred years of detention and Mr. Hernandez mutating into a black hole of vengeance.

But Mr. Hernandez only made me run twenty laps of the football field.

I blame myself for not communicating properly to the student body, Rafe. If you thought I was a weird alien-type pod person, that's got to be at least partly my fault. Now, go run a few laps, and we'll say no more about it.

Yeah, right. And that happened.

Like I said—*weird*. And I haven't even gotten to the drop bears yet.

CHAPTER 3

BUDGIE SMUGGLERS, AHOY!

Later that day, things got even weirder. The school had a special assembly, and after Principal Stricker droned on for, like, ten minutes, she introduced the mayor of Hills Village.

Mayor Blitz Coogan is one of those big, nice, friendly guys who slap everyone on the back in a big, nice, friendly way with their gigantic paws. He gave Principal Stricker such a big, nice, friendly pat on the back that she almost coughed up a lung and crowd-surfed off the stage.

"G'day, Hills Village!" Mayor Coogan boomed into the microphone. "Fair dinkum, it's a bonzer arvo for you and yer cobbers to put on the old budgie smugglers and take the planks down the beach to catch a couple of goofy breaks out back!"

There was a stunned silence.

Other than the words "Hills Village," nothing Mayor Coogan had said made any sense. We looked at him like he'd lost his mind. Mayor Coogan just stood there smiling like a guy who'd won the lottery.

"That's what folks in Australia speak like! I just got back from a trip to Shark's Bay, Australia, where my brother, Biff, lives. And I've got some very exciting news." Mayor Coogan paused again like he was announcing the winner of a national TV talent show. "Hills Village is now *twinned* with Shark's Bay!"

Mayor Coogan beamed a big smile that made him look like a xylophone was lodged in his mouth, and glanced expectantly around the auditorium like he was waiting for the applause to die down. The only problem was that there wasn't any, other than a few stray claps from the teachers.

The only way it could have been any worse was if his pants had fallen down.

"Twinning," Mayor Coogan continued, "means that our two towns are now special partners that will learn a lot from each other. It's all about reaching out, sharing ideas, and cultural exchange."

It all sounded so boring I almost passed out.

Until something Mayor Coogan said jolted me out of my drooly daydream.

"...and first prize in the Shark's Bay/Hills Village Art Competition will be a three-week, all-expenses-paid trip to Australia. Judging takes place next week. Get creative, Hills Village, and you could be on that plane!"

Art, I thought. *I can do art.*

I could win that prize! I bet Mom would like that A LOT.

Mostly because my trouble in middle school has been hard on Mom, too. HVMS has a rule book so big that it requires two grown men to open it—and I'm not exactly great at following the rules. So, naturally, I got expelled at one point. Mom wasn't too pleased.

You can see why I could use a fresh start, at least in Mom's eyes. Winning Mayor Coogan's art competition could give me another chance to make it up to her.

Well, *another* another chance.

Reasons to enter the art competition

① Three whole weeks of no school.

② Three whole weeks away from Georgia.

③ Three whole weeks without Miller the killer.

④ Three whole weeks for Jeanne Galletta to realize how much she misses me.

⑤ I get to go to Australia.

But if I was such a good artist and I had a shot at a free trip Down Under, and if winning that trip would make Mom proud of me, why did I have a feeling in my stomach like I'd just swallowed an octopus?

CHAPTER 4

FAIR TRADE

Mayor Coogan's speech lasted longer than the last ice age, so I'll condense it down to the bare bones.

He explained that Shark's Bay was a surfing town north of Sydney. The idea was that the winner of the art competition would live there for three weeks and create artwork inspired by Australian culture, then exhibit it at a special party. An Australian artist would come over to Hills Village to do the same thing. Now, I had no idea what Shark's Bay was like, and I didn't want to diss my own hometown, but *that* didn't sound like much of a trade for the other side.

An expert panel—Mayor Blitz Coogan, Ms. Donatello (the Hills Village Middle School art teacher), and Earl O'Reilly of Earl's Auto (the sponsor of the prize)—would make the decision.

After the assembly, someone tapped me on the shoulder. It was Ms. Donatello.

"You should give it a shot," she said. "I think you have a real chance, Rafe."

Ms. Donatello is always doing stuff like that. She's a bit like my mom—saying I can do things even when I'm not too sure I can. She really believes in me. It kind of freaks me out, but in a good way.

"Don't you want a free trip to Australia?"

Um, YES! Who *wouldn't* want a free trip to Australia?

Beaches, sun, shrimps on the barbie, palm trees…uh…kangaroos. But even though Ms. Donatello had a good point, that octopus in my guts was still sloshing around like crazy.

And I knew exactly why.

It was all thanks to the Discovery Channel.

CHAPTER 5

KILLER FRUIT

Flashback to three days earlier, a Friday night. My absolute favorite night of the week, and I was practicing my favorite pastime: playing my TrollQuest video game with a bag of corn chips balanced on my knee for easy snack-cess. I'm pretty good at it.

Georgia was out doing little-sister stuff somewhere with her little-sister friends, and Mom had the night off from work, so she was making something tasty-smelling in the kitchen. I settled into the cushions, put my feet up, and switched on the TV.

"Doesn't get much better than this, hmm, Leo?" I shoveled another fistful of Tastee Taco Shells into my mouth as I heaved a boulder onto some troll-eating maggots. Leo didn't say anything. He had a mouthful of Tastee Taco Shells. Plus, he's not real.

These days he mostly sticks to showing up in my drawings. I mean, it's not like I'm *completely* nuts. Not yet, anyway.

After I finished my TrollQuest level, I flipped on a Discovery Channel special about—you guessed it—Australia. It was *great*. Apparently, everything in Australia is dangerous. Everything. And when I say everything, I mean *everything* everything.

Even the flowers are toxic. *Flowers.*

The Lilshopohorroria (aka: The Pink Terminator)

There's a fruit that tastes like paradise but contains vicious barbed hooks that latch on to the soft part of your throat, causing you to die. HOOKS! What possible reason could there be for a tasty fruit to contain killer throat hooks?

And the Irukandji, the world's most venomous jellyfish, lives in Australia. The thing looks like an evil, transparent gummy bear.

They have birds that could *kill* you.

Why would a giant bird need claws? It makes no sense. The cassowary can't even fly. It has these little stunted wings.

Wouldn't it have been a better idea for the cassowaries to grow some actual wings and leave the claws and sprinting to the cheetahs?

Creature after creature rolled on-screen, each of them even more fearsome, more bloodthirsty, or just plain weirder than the last. Crocodiles as big as school buses, Tasmanian devils (don't ask), goannas (basically dinosaurs), ghost bats (of course), stonefish (deadly fish sneakily disguised as stones), poisonous blue-ringed octopuses (cute little octopuses that are possibly the most poisonous creatures on the planet), venomous snakes by the bucketload, redback spiders, scorpions, stick insects (so big they should be called log insects), killer caterpillars (*caterpillars!*), toadfish (with teeth shaped like a parrot's beak that are capable of ripping off your toe)…and sharks.

Lots and lots and lots of sharks. Tiger sharks, bull sharks, makos, hammerheads, blues, and the big daddy of them all—the shark that gives me nightmares—the great white.

Nothing on earth could have ever persuaded me to set foot in Australia.

"They have sharks in America, too, dummy," Leo said.

"Not in Hills Village, they don't," I replied.

It was like the whole ecosystem had been designed by a complete nutzoid with a really twisted sense of humor. As far as I could tell, Australia was basically an island full of monsters.

"Man, that is one scary place!" I muttered, and switched the channel to something more soothing—a show about a friendly neighborhood serial killer.

CHAPTER 6

THAT OLD DONATELLO CHARM

O kay, so we've established that there was absolutely no way, no how, no chance on this earth that I would ever even *think* about entering the Shark's Bay/Hills Village Art Competition.

And on Tuesday morning that's exactly what I didn't do—*think*.

Without knowing why (and most likely because Ms. Donatello used some kind of sneaky alien brainwashing device), I found myself bundling up my best drawings and my sketchbook, putting them into a folder, taking them in to school, walking to the judging room, and submitting my drawings to the art competition committee.

As I closed the door on my way out, everything seemed to get sharper and clearer, as though the

entire morning had taken place underwater. Ms.
Donatello's secret brainwashing device must have
been more powerful than I realized.

It doesn't really matter, though, I thought on my way back to class. There was no way on earth I'd win. Stuff like that doesn't happen to me. Rafe Khatchadorian is the kid who gets busted, the kid who messes things up, the kid who's stalked by Miller the Killer through the halls of Hills Village, the kid who, above everything else, *fails.*

But maybe there was an alignment of the planets or something, because...*I won.*

That's right.

A trip to Australia, all expenses paid! An exhibition in Shark's Bay! Best of all, THREE WEEKS OFF FROM SCHOOL!

Khatchadorian shoots! He scores! He *WINS!* Is there *anything* this kid can't do?

And then I remembered something. Something that terrified me. Something that threw a 2,400-pound wrench in my plans. Something that meant the trip Down Under would definitely *not* be happening.

"You're remembering the sharks, aren't you?" Leo said. Leo is sharp like that. He always knows exactly what I'm thinking, which isn't that surprising, since he lives inside my head.

"Uh-huh," I said. "And the snakes and spiders and crocodiles and jellyfish and octopuses." I shivered.

Leo shrugged. "You could always stay out of the ocean."

I was about to say what a dumb idea *that* was when I realized that Leo was right. I *could* stay out of the ocean! I couldn't remember hearing about anyone being eaten by a great white while skateboarding on *land*. Staying out of the ocean would reduce my chances of being chomped by at least 100 percent. I liked those odds a whole lot better. It would mean abandoning my plans to learn how to surf, but sometimes you can't have everything.

"The snakes and spiders probably aren't as bad as the Discovery Channel says," Leo said. "TV exaggerates things, like, a million billion times."

Leo was right again. I *was* probably making too much of the creepy-crawlies. I mean, they were just *bugs*. (Well, they might be bugs the size of a spaniel, and they might carry enough venom to knock out a polar bear, but they were still just bugs.) And besides, what was the chance I'd actually get bitten by a venomous snake or accidentally eat a poisonous fruit?

"If you still think Australia's too scary, you could always say no," Leo said. "Give back the prize."

Give back the prize? I froze. Leo had a point. A really *stupid* point.

"Are you out of your mind?" I yelled. "I *won* something! Me! There's no way I'm handing that back. Are you kidding? *Australia,* dude! Sun, beaches, first-class plane tickets, surfing, girls, koala bears, the Sydney Harbor Bridge, my very own exhibition, the Opera House!"

"Because you really like opera."

"I'm on a roll, Leo, and the only thing you can do when you're on a roll is—"

"Put butter on it?"

"Go with the flow!"

Leo looked puzzled. "How does that work? Going with the flow and being on a roll? Like, wouldn't you—"

"Don't worry about all that! I won. We're going. Things are finally going right for Rafe Khatchadorian!"

RANDOM READER

WHOA! HEY! STOP RIGHT THERE! TIME OUT! TIME! OUT!

Whoa, whoa, whoa, hold up, Khatchadorian. How is it that five minutes ago you were yelling about sharks and spiders and all that stuff, then— *bingo!*—you're suddenly rolling over like a puppy getting its tummy rubbed and accepting the prize? What gives?

I'll tell you what gives: success!

It's not something I've had much of these past few years, and now that things were going well for me—for once—I wasn't about to let opportunity pass me by. I'm not *that* stupid.

Besides, people were noticing me now more than ever. Jeanne Galletta said I looked "happy" in math class yesterday. Me! Happy in math class!

Earl O'Reilly, the contest's sponsor, told Mom that Hills Village was very proud of me and that he was sure I'd do a great job of representing us in Austria and that I should get some good skiing in while I was over there. (I think Earl may have some work to do on his geography skills.) The *Hills*

Village Sentinel was even planning to do a story on me. I'm officially in the big leagues, baby!

Of all the reasons for going to Australia, though, the best one was the look on my mom's face when I told her I won the contest. She was smiling so much that I thought her face would break.

"Rafe, you're amazing!" she yelled, and gave me a great big embarrassing Mom Hug right in the middle of Swifty's, the diner she works at. "My own little Picasso!"

And the sharks? I guess I'll figure that out once I get there.

CHAPTER 7

MUTANT ALBATROSS FEATHERS

I should have known there'd be a catch. A big Mom-shaped catch.

"*Of course* I'm coming with you. If you think they'd let someone your age fly halfway around the world and hang out in a foreign country alone, then you have another think coming, mister!"

Well, you could have knocked me down with a feather. In fact, just as Mom doled out this shocking news, a feather from a passing mutant albatross hit me on the shoulder and I went down like a boxer in the tenth round. KO!

Okay, I might be exaggerating a little—in the sense that it didn't actually happen—but you have to cut me some slack here. Finding out that Mom was coming with me Down Under was a big blow!

When you're my age, going *anywhere* with your mom—even if she's an awesome one like mine—is about as uncool as you can possibly get. Did I really think she'd let me fly solo halfway around the world and hang out alone in a foreign country doing exactly what I wanted, when I wanted, and where I wanted?

You bet!

So when Mom broke the news that she was going to be coming with me, I didn't lie around whining—I stood up and did my whining like a man! I whined in the living room, I whined in the dining room, and I whined in the kitchen. I whined before breakfast and I whined at dinner.

I whined from dawn till dusk with hardly a break for breathing. I whined like no kid has ever whined before.

And I didn't restrict myself to whining. I moaned, pleaded, begged, sulked, shouted, and whimpered...all of which produced exactly zero results. I even pulled out my secret weapon—the patented full-beam Khatchadorian Death Stare, which has been known to laser a hole in two-inch titanium—but Mom just asked me if I had something in my eye and told me to quit blocking the TV.

THE KHATCHADORIAN DEATH STARE

Eventually, by the night before the trip, I got used to the idea of Mom coming with me to Australia. It wasn't like I was happy about it, but I moved on from whine to whatever.

After a restless night plagued by crocodile-infested dreams, I woke at dawn. I already felt jet-lagged and I hadn't even gotten out of bed.

ME

I'll spare you all the details about Mom wailing like a wounded whale when she said good-bye to Georgia and Grandma Dotty at the airport. It was gross. There was enough salt water splashing around to fill the Hills Village Municipal Swimming Pool, with plenty left over. But finally, after fifty million hugs and sniffles, we were all set to board the plane. That's when we found out that Earl O'Reilly and Mayor Coogan didn't exactly go premium on the plane tickets.

Welcome to Aussie AirWays, mates! I'm your captain, Ryan "Mad Dog" Porter. Today we'll be cruising at an altitude of, like, real high. Due to the lack of space on board, there will be no meals served, but the cabin crew will hurl bags of stale peanuts at you, and you can fight it out among yourselves...

But despite the super-cramped seats and the bumpy ride, and despite Mom coming along, I decided I was just going to enjoy this free vacation to the other side of the world. I wedged myself into the window seat and watched the Pacific unfurl below me. I was a new Rafe Khatchadorian, a globe-trotting, internationally famous artist.

What could possibly go wrong?

CHAPTER 8

THE BEAST

I was right on the crest of the Beast—a wave so big that some of the surf pros were having second thoughts about going back out into the swells again.

But not me. I waved to them as they stared at me from shore, amazed at my graceful glide along the craziest wave they'd ever seen. One cute surfer girl waved back, so I did a quick backflip to show her that I wasn't afraid. That's when the Beast rose even higher and started crashing down over me, pulling me under and—**PING!**

Hey! I'm just big-boned!

The seat belt light went on and I woke up sweating like a hot-sauce-slurping pig in a sauna.

"Quit moving around so much," Mom hissed, clutching my arm. "You'll make the plane wobble."

Did I mention she's not a good flyer? Actually, she is possibly the Most Nervous Passenger in the History of Flying.

I glanced at her tray table. Spread out across it was a rabbit's foot, a four-leaf clover, a Bible, a copy of the Koran, a sprig of heather, a string of prayer beads, a silver cross of Saint Christopher, two barf bags, a "lucky" pebble shaped like Minnesota that she had found in the yard, a booklet about the plane's safety features, a bottle of motion-sickness pills, a book by Dr. Enrique Meloma titled *Don't Freak Out at 35,000 Feet Ever Again!*, and a laminated picture of the Dalai Lama.

I looked out of the window and immediately forgot all about my dream. The plane was coming in low over a perfect blue sea. We were arriving in Australia and it was all I could do to stay in my seat.

As we touched down and coasted alongside a strip of trees that lined the edge of the bay, I pressed my nose against the window and caught a glimpse of something furry moving in the upper branches. I looked closer and saw a flash of light as the sun winked off the creature's eyes. I swear it was staring at me.

"Did you see that?" I said to Mom, but she had her eyes screwed shut and her hands clamped so tightly on the armrests that it was a miracle they weren't broken yet. "Mom! I saw something in the trees!"

A deep voice came from behind my left shoulder and I jumped about six feet. It was the man in the row behind me, leaning forward.

"You saw something, son?" he said with a strong Australian accent. His face was leathery brown, and his blond hair was graying at the sides. He had the air of a man who wrestled crocodiles for fun.

I nodded. "In the trees."

"Drop bears," the man said gravely.

I saw the woman next to him glance at him quickly. "Terry...," she said.

"The boy's got to know, Shirl," the man said in a voice that came all the way from down in his boots. "He's a visitor to our country."

Shirl shook her head and turned back to her magazine.

The man leaned forward as the plane taxied toward the terminal. His voice dropped to a whisper. "That was a drop bear you saw, son."

"A drop bear?" I said. "I've never heard of them."

"Exactly. That's what they want," the man replied. "Drop bears are the most dangerous animals in Australia. They call 'em koalas to throw you off the trail. I used to hunt them on the Sydney Harbor Bridge. Every night they'd climb up there and cling to the steel—they like the warmth, you see—and every now and again one would drop down to hunt. They kill hundreds every year. Just drop down and rip out their brains while they're still alive. Horrible, it is, just horrible."

"Hundreds of what?" I gasped. "What do they kill?" The Discovery Channel had obviously missed something in its research.

There was a pause before he spoke, like he was weighing whether or not to give me some very bad news. "Tourists," the man growled. "They feed on tourists, son."

Oh, no.

I was a tourist.

"That's enough, Terry," Shirl said.

The plane came to a halt and the FASTEN SEAT BELT sign pinged off.

Terry unbuckled his seat belt, his face grim. "You take care, sonny," he said. "Watch the skies and remember to take precautions."

"What sort of precautions?" I asked, but he was already gone.

CHAPTER 9

SHE'LL BE RIGHT, MATE

Australia is hot.

Like, REALLY hot. Frying-eggs-on-the-sidewalk hot. Ice-cream-melting-before-you-can-take-the-first-lick hot. Did I mention it was hot?

Is it me or is it hot in here?

It was so hot that all thoughts of drop bears vanished immediately. Having my brains sucked out and eaten would be the least of my problems. I'd be boiled alive *long* before that happened.

Hey, Hills Village has its hot days—plenty of them—but there was one small but VERY important detail I'd forgotten. While it was winter back home, here in Upside-Down Land it was most definitely summer. And I was still wearing my winter clothes.

"This is nice," Mom said, smiling.

I looked at her like she'd gone crazy. Somehow, between leaving the plane and getting outside, and without me noticing a thing, she'd magically changed into light summer clothes. How do they *do* that? Moms, I mean.

"Nice?" I said. *"Nice?"*

I'd expected Australia to be warm, but this was something else. People needed Special Forces training to deal with this kind of thing. How did Australians stop themselves from melting? Did they have some sort of force field? Ice water running through their veins? Skin like elephant hide? Whatever it was, I needed to find out—and soon.

To make matters worse, the airline lost our bags.

"Once we find 'em, we'll send 'em up to Shark's Bay," the smiling, blond, surfer-type guy said from behind the desk. "She'll be right, mate."

I have no idea what "She'll be right, mate" means, but I'm guessing it's something like "I have absolutely no idea what the outcome of this problem might be, up to and including injury and/or death, but I'm blindly hoping that things will turn out for the best." Never trust an Australian who says this to you, as I've learned. And, no, I don't know why it's always "she" who'll be right and not "he." It just is.

What I found out in Australia was that quite often things did not turn out right, but—and this is the important thing to remember—it never stopped Australians from *saying* they would. Be warned.

Plus, we found out that the trip north to Shark's Bay was going to take SEVEN HOURS.

On a bus with a malfunctioning air conditioner. Seven.

HOURS.

A TV at the front of the bus was switched to the news. The grinning anchorman proudly told us that Australia was experiencing one of the hottest days on record, with the mercury nudging 46 degrees Celsius. The guy sounded like that was something to boast about.

"That's 115 degrees Fahrenheit!" I gasped. "Seven hours without air-conditioning?" I asked the driver.

"She'll be right, mate," he replied, smiling like a hyena with a caffeine problem.

See?

I'll spare you most of the horrible details of our journey.

All you need to know is that at one point a bug as big as a bear flew across my face and, instead of screaming like a normal person, I was just grateful for the breeze.

When we arrived at our first rest stop, I staggered down the steps of the bus. Wherever we'd stopped was hotter than Sydney. I was literally melting.

I was about

to complain, but after seeing Mom's scary jet-lagged expression, I stopped melting and got back on the bus without a word.

At least I didn't see any more drop bears in the trees. It was probably too hot, even for them.

CHAPTER 10

THUNDER DOWN UNDER

When the bus arrived in Shark's Bay, the boiling day had curdled into a full-scale thunderstorm. Rain of biblical proportions hammered down on the roof of the bus.

I gazed out the window and nudged Mom. "Look at that."

Outside, palm trees were bending in the wind. It was like the news footage you see when Channel 2 is reporting a Category 5 storm from Miami or Haiti. I saw a small car tumbling through the air, followed by a pizza shop and what looked like a whole herd of cows.

Okay, I made that last part up. But it did look bad.

"I hope it's not a hurricane," Mom said. She leaned forward and tapped the driver on the shoulder. "This isn't a hurricane or something we should be worried about, is it?" She paused, then added, "We're American."

"Nah, just a bit of a breeze," the bus driver said. "Anyway, we don't believe in hurricanes. In Australia, we have cyclones."

"Isn't a cyclone just another name for a hurricane?" I asked.

My Friday nights in front of the Discovery Channel had included plenty of shows on typhoons, tsunamis, hurricanes, and tornadoes. I was an expert at this point.

"Nah," the driver said, looking at me as if I was nuts. "*Totally* different thing. She'll be right, mate."

"What about those hailstones?" Mom said.

"Those itty-bitty little specks of ice? Completely flamin' harmless! Now get off me flamin' bus, ya drongos!"

The bus driver
skidded to a halt in what looked
like the parking lot of a fried-
chicken joint. The hail was coming
down hard and quick, so we made
a run for a bus shelter. We had gone
from superhot to ice-cold in less than two
minutes. We were clearly in the middle of
some enormous natural disaster. The best
we could hope for was that our waterlogged bodies
would be found wedged in the branches of a tree a
week later during the massive cleanup operation.

Over the noise of the hailstones hammering
down, Mom told me that Mayor Coogan's brother,
Biff, was supposed to meet us. I leaned against a
graffiti-covered wall and looked out at the curtain
of hail.

"This isn't what I imagined," I said, but Mom
wasn't listening.

She was fast asleep.

CHAPTER 11

CHUNDER DOWN UNDER

After what seemed like hours but was actually six minutes and eighteen seconds, a car screeched into the parking lot and slid to a halt in front of the bus shelter. A six-foot-tall chicken sprang out of the driver's seat and stood looking at us as hailstones the size of tennis balls bounced off his head as though they were made of popcorn. Mom and I stared back.

Maybe the hail *was* popcorn. Nothing would surprise me about Australia anymore. For all I knew, the hailstones contained exploding poison darts, or possessed claws, or six sets of fangs. Everything

else in this country seemed to have unnecessary protective armor.

Or the chicken possibly had a head made of solid granite.

Either way, he didn't seem to notice.

The chicken's car, on the other hand, took a beating. I watched the left side-view mirror get caught by a particularly large hailstone and crash to the ground. Ice *rat-a-tat-tat*ed the roof, and the windshield cracked in three places. The chicken didn't seem to mind. Maybe these giant chickens had plenty of spare cars.

"G'day, you blokes!" the chicken boomed. He lifted his wings and pulled off his head to reveal someone who looked very much like Blitz Coogan. "Biff Coogan's the name, and I'm mayor of this joint!" Biff Coogan pointed at his chicken suit. "I don't normally dress like this, but me and Mrs. Coogan have got a fancy-dress party coming up, and I've just been to pick up my costume. Thought I'd leave it on and give you a bit of a laugh!"

"Fancy-dress"? "A bit of a laugh"? It was obvious he'd lived in Australia a long time. Any trace of American in his voice was gone. He even sounded more Australian than any of the Australians we had met so far. At least I could still understand him, though. It could be worse—he could be speaking Chicken.

"Ha, ha," I said, doing my best to appear amused.

It seemed to satisfy Biff.

"What about your car?" I asked. "It's getting totally destroyed."

Biff glanced at the car. "Oh, that's not mine. It's Mrs. Coogan's. My car had a bit of a run-in with the hailstones, but this car's a beaut. She'll—"

"Let me guess," I said. "She'll be right, mate?"

"You got it, buddy," said Biff. "We'll make an Aussie of you yet!"

He stepped forward and shook Mom's hand.

"Ha!" she said. "I mean, hi. Ny mane'th Rafe and this son is my Jules. I mean, my name's Rafejools and this son is my. Wait, what I mean..."

She may have been *trying* to look like she wasn't auditioning for a role in a zombie flick, but she definitely wasn't succeeding. She sounded as if her tongue had been replaced by a drowsy ferret. I began to wonder about those travel pills she'd been popping on the plane. She *had* mentioned something about side effects...

Biff didn't seem to notice.

"No worries, Rafejools! Welcome to Australia!" Biff opened the doors to what was left of Mrs. Coogan's car. "Pity we couldn't have fixed up some sun for you guys. Okay, let's go!"

We made a death-defying leap through the hail and into the relative safety of the backseat. The hail sounded even louder inside the car than when we were standing under the bus shelter. Biff looked around the front seat at us.

"You blokes are traveling light!" he yelled.

I didn't bother explaining. I was too tired. Our luggage would turn up or it wouldn't. After twenty-six hours on the move, plus a sleepless night before that, I didn't care if the bags ended up in Saskatchewan.

I sat back and watched as we drove through town. A sign read WELCOME TO SHARK'S BAY, AUSTRALIA'S MOST FEARLESS TOWN.

"'Most Fearless'?" I said. "What's that all about?"

"Shark's Bay surfers," Biff replied. "We got sharks here in Shark's Bay—lots of sharks—but that never stops a Shark's Bay surfer!"

I gulped and exchanged a meaningful look with Leo.

"Did he say 'lots'?" Leo asked.

I nodded.

"Oh, boy."

"But don't worry," Biff said, "hardly anyone gets eaten. Heh, heh, heh."

"Great," I muttered. "How far to the hotel?"

All I wanted was a shower and a bed I could sleep in for, say, three weeks straight.

"Oh, you'll be staying at our little beach shack," Biff said as he swerved around a fallen tree in the middle of the road. He turned in his seat and grinned. "More cozy than a hotel, hey?"

I sat up and looked at Leo.

A *shack?* That hadn't been part of the deal. I'd thought it'd be some swanky five-star resort, not some complete stranger's backyard shed.

"I didn't know about *this!*" I hissed.

"Of course, Rafe," Mom said. She had a strange, glassy expression on her face, and her skin looked a bit green.

"I mean, we don't know these people!"

"Mmm, yeah, apples," Mom said, nodding. Her

eyes wobbled in different directions. "And oranges. Christmas stockings."

I looked at her. "Mom, are you okay?"

"What a strange question, Rafe. Of course I'm Wednesday."

And then, before anyone could stop her, Mom leaned forward and did the unthinkable.

She puked.

All over the back of Biff Coogan's head.

It was a full-on, pedal-to-the-metal puke tornado, too, not a measly quarter or half hurl. It was the real deal, chunks blown, projectile Vom City to the maximillion. It was messy. It was loud. It was *spewtastic!*

It was probably the single most awesome thing I'd ever seen.

CHAPTER 12

BiFFZiLLA VERSUS MOM

Everyone froze. In fact, as you can imagine, the atmosphere inside the car cooled down right away. The temperature dropped so much you could have used the inside of the car as a training pod for an Antarctic expedition.

"Whoa," I said. It seemed to sum up the situation.

Getting puked on by a complete stranger can't be much fun. Getting puked on by a complete stranger while dressed in a chicken suit must have been much, much worse.

And funnier, too, although a big part of me felt really (like, *really*) bad for Mom. *She couldn't help it,* I wanted to say. Maybe I should've explained to Biff that a combination of jet lag, heat, travel pills, and an Aussie Airways tuna bake had combined to turn my nice, polite mom into a walking puke machine, but Biff didn't look like he wanted anyone to talk to him, least of all me.

But, I thought, my hopes rising, *we're in Australia.* They had a different sense of humor compared with the rest of the world. They were used to sharks and snakes and poisonous flowers. Maybe being puked on was regarded as a bit of harmless fun here.

No such luck. Biff wasn't giving even the slightest hint that any part of being puked on came within the same solar system as being fun.

And—this is just a hunch—Mom puking on

the mayor was probably the wrong way to start a cultural exchange. Right now, the chances of Hills Village and Shark's Bay becoming best buds looked about as likely as me playing the saxophone on the moon.

"I. Am. So. So. So. *So.* Sorry," Mom said. "*Really* sorry, Mayor Coogan. I couldn't help it."

She started trying to wipe the worst of the gunge off Biff's neck but only managed to accidentally slide a chunky gloop of it right down the back of his chicken costume.

Biff squirmed out of her reach. He yanked a box of tissues toward him and began wiping the puke off by himself. Disregarding the hurricane outside, I rolled down the window to let in some fresh air. I was beginning to feel a little pukey myself, and I didn't think Biff would appreciate a repeat performance. Being puked on once is bad enough.

"She's been taking some travel pills," I shouted above the howling gale filling the car. "That must be it."

"If it's any consolation," Mom said, "I do feel a lot better now." Then she closed her eyes and fell fast asleep.

A low rumbling noise, like someone dragging a heavy anchor over concrete, filled the car. At first I thought we'd hit something and lost a tire and the noise was the wheel scraping across the road, but then I realized it was Biff grinding his teeth. He was the angriest-looking giant chicken I'd ever seen.

He didn't say anything, but I could tell by the vicious twist he gave the steering wheel to avoid a speedboat resting upside down in the middle of an intersection that he was about a millisecond away from turning around and putting us on the next bus back to Sydney. One more incident and I had no doubt that he'd mutate into Biffzilla, and the whole Shark's Bay/Hills Village twin experiment would turn into a massive disaster.

I imagined slinking back home, a failure once again. It wasn't a good thought.

"Maybe we should take her to the hospital," Biff said when he had finally unclenched his puke-spotted jaw.

"Nah," I replied. "She'll be right, mate."

I couldn't resist.

IN THE BIG HOUSE

The moment we arrived, the hail suddenly stopped. It was like someone had thrown a switch, and the clouds were split open by a beam of sunlight that lit up the place like a stage spotlight. I half expected a choir of angels to start singing. But we were in for an even bigger shock: the Coogans' "shack" sprawled across a huge chunk of land that wrapped around half of Shark's Bay. Being a mayor must pay pretty well, because I'd seen airports that were smaller than Biff Coogan's beach shack.

In the driveway, a tall blond kid about my age stopped doing ollies on his skateboard and stared at me.

It wasn't a friendly look. His eyes reminded me of the drop bear's.

"Bradley, this is Ralph Katchadoorhandle," Biff said as he stepped out of the car. "Ralph, this is my son, Bradley. He's on school break right now."

"Eww!" Bradley said, pointing at his dad's puke-encrusted neck. "What in the name of Hugh Jackman's sideburns is *that* gunk?"

Biff shook his head and stomped toward the house.

"That's, uh, puke," I said.

"You puked on Dad? Why?"

"No! My mom puked on your dad," I said, like that made it okay.

Bradley looked at me and then at Mom in the car. "But she's asleep."

"No," I said. "Well, yes, she is now. But she wasn't then, so she could have. And did. Puke, I mean."

Nope, still not getting it, I am.

To be honest, it wasn't the clearest

answer I'd ever given. Even I could hardly understand it. But I was way too tired and hungry and smelly to think even a little bit clearly.

Bradley opened his mouth to speak and then closed it again. You could almost see his brain trying to work out the sequence of events.

"Okay," he managed in the end. A blond girl who looked a lot like Bradley appeared next to him.

"What's *that?*" she said, pointing at me like I was some sort of exotic slug.

Bradley shrugged. "Some American dude," he said. "Puked all over the old bloke. Fair dinkum."

"Ew, gross!"

"I didn't!" I protested.

"This is my twin sister, Belinda," Bradley said.

Belinda looked at me briefly again and shook her head.

I wanted to tell her how tired we were and that it wasn't me who had puked on her dad, but I didn't have the energy. Instead, I opened my mouth and, without warning, puked all over Belinda.

CHAPTER 14

BeeTS?

Let's just say that Belinda took being puked on a lot worse than her dad.

For a moment there I thought she was going to smack me with Bradley's skateboard, but her desire to clean my puke off her T-shirt was too great. Belinda fled into the house, swearing undying hatred and vengeance against me in particular and Americans in general.

I didn't blame her. I would have felt exactly the same way if a random Australian had showed up in Hills Village and hurled chunks all over me.

Bradley, on the other hand, thought it was the funniest thing he'd ever seen.

"Awesome." Bradley chuckled. He jumped onto his skateboard and disappeared down the driveway.

A few minutes later, after I'd woken Mom up and gotten her out of the car, Mrs. Coogan stepped out the door. She must have heard all about the puky Americans, because I noticed she stayed a few paces out of hurl range.

Barb wasted no time showing us to our rooms and demonstrating exactly how the showers worked.

"Take your time," she said.

WHAT BARB REALLY MEANT...

YOU STINK! GET CLEANED UP!

Thirty minutes later, showered and changed and feeling a little more like our old selves, we came downstairs to eat. I imagined that we'd be eating giant cockroaches cooked on the barbie or something, but we had regular steaks and burgers and fries and salad. The only weird thing was the beets Mrs. Coogan insisted on putting on the burgers. *Beets*.

Belinda didn't speak to me. I don't even know if it would have been any different if I *hadn't* puked on her. I tried to apologize, but she just ignored me.

A bunch of Bradley and Belinda's friends came over for dinner. They were just like the twins—all big white teeth and blond hair and tans. Too good-looking, too tall, and too well dressed. Frankly, Bradley and Belinda Coogan and all their friends were just too *perfect* to be human. (The pod people strike again!)

I think Mrs. Coogan thought having Bradley and Belinda's friends there would make it easier for me to befriend them. But that idea was definitely *not* going to work. I hated Bradley and Belinda's friends on sight, and they hated me. It looked like I wasn't going to be warmly welcomed

THE REAL BRADLEY AND BELINDA!

into the Shark's Bay surfer community anytime soon, but I was so tired I didn't care. I just hoped that not everyone in Australia would be like Bradley and Belinda's crew.

By eight o'clock I could feel my eyes drooping, and Mom must have felt the same. We made our excuses and crawled to our rooms.

"Sleep tight, Rafe," Mom said as she closed her door.

I muttered something back, but it may as well have been in Swahili. All I could think about was sleep, glorious sleep.

Less than thirty seconds later, I slid between the sheets of my bed, closed my eyes, and dropped into the deepest sleep of my life.

CHAPTER 15

THE ROPE OF DOOM

There's *no* sleep like jet-lag sleep. It was like being under anesthesia. I sank into the soft, billowing pillows, which soon turned into soft, billowing clouds, and then I was gone. For a time, there was just velvety blackness, and then I began to dream I was tightrope-walking across a river. It wasn't a bad dream—the tightrope was wide and fat and warm beneath my feet. I wrapped my toes around the rope and kept walking.

The only trouble was that the wind started rising, and the rope began moving up and down and from side to side. It became harder and harder for me to cling on, so I reached down and wrapped my arms tight around that rope and hung on as if my life depended on it. The rope was moving so much that it was wrapping itself around my legs and—

"This is not a drill, soldier! Mayday! I repeat, Mayday!"

Leo's voice cut through my dream like a chain saw. My eyes popped open, but I couldn't see a thing in the darkened room. After a moment, I realized that the tightrope was still moving.

That's weird, I thought. The tightrope was in my dream, wasn't it? How could it still be moving?

"The lights!" Leo screamed. "Hit the lights!"

I reached across and fumbled for the bedside lamp. My finger found the switch, and I realized that the *thing* coiled around my feet and legs wasn't a tightrope.

It was a giant SNAKE!

CHAPTER 16

REVENGE OF THE POD PEOPLE

You know the movie *Snakes on a Plane*? This was *Snake in the Bed*. Much, much, *much* scarier. Mainly because it was happening to me in REAL LIFE and not to Samuel L. Jackson on a Hollywood movie set.

The snake and I stared at each other and time seemed to stop. Then, at incredible speed, a number of things happened all at once.

Brainy scientists say that it is aerodynamically impossible for a human being to fly. The laws of physics do not allow it.

And what I would say to those scientists is this: Quit flapping your gums, Einsteins. You might know plenty about science and mathematics, but you don't know what a human is capable of when

he finds a snake in his bed. But if you wanted to conduct an experiment to find out, all you'd have to do is place one terrified kid (for the sake of argument, let's call him Rafe Khatchadorian) in close proximity to a giant snake, and you would see unaided human flight take place in about two seconds flat. Guaranteed.

Once I had computed the impossible information that there was, in fact, a huge snake in my bed, I levitated so fast that I bounced off the ceiling, spun around in midair, and rocketed out of the room at approximately 926 miles an hour without my feet touching the ground once.

Did I mention I was screaming?

Well, I was—loudly and without drawing breath and in a voice so high I was surprised the windows didn't shatter. As soon as I locked eyes on the reptile in my bed, I screamed like a police siren without an Off switch.

I screamed as I hurtled down the Coogans' hallway, I screamed as I clattered down the stairs, and I was still screaming as I sprinted into the crowded living room, tripped over a coffee table, and somersaulted into the TV, which exploded in a totally impressive shower of sparks and smoke. I was left sprawled half over the coffee table, with cake all over me, my butt stuck up high in the air, and my face buried in the carpet.

It wasn't a good look.

See?

"SNNNNNNAAAAAAAAAAAAAAKKKKE!" I howled, lifting my chin from the carpet. "S-S-S-S-S-S-S-S-S-SNAAAAAAAAAAKKKKKE!"

There was a moment of stunned silence. Biff and Barb Coogan looked blankly at me and then at the busted TV.

"Snake?" I said. My voice went up at the end of the word like I was asking a question. Maybe I *was* asking a question. Maybe there hadn't been a snake?

And then Bradley and Belinda and all their surfy-alien-mutant friends started to laugh. They laughed until tears ran down their perfect cheeks. They would stop laughing for a second and then see my yellow underwear with the stars and start laughing all over again.

"Stop," one kid gasped, holding his hands up. "I can't breathe!" And then he rolled over, his shoulders shaking.

They'd stop laughing, and then someone would say, "The TV!" and off they'd go once more. If one of them had literally laughed their head right off their shoulders, I wouldn't have been surprised.

Even Biff and Barb joined in.

Then Mom arrived. "What's all the noise?" she asked.

"Rafe's making us all laugh," Barb Coogan said. "He's quite a joker, isn't he?"

Before Mom could reply, Bradley turned to one of his friends. "You get that, Danny?" he said.

I looked around to see Bradley's friend holding up his phone and nodding. "Every last freakin' second, Bradster," he said. He leaned forward and high-fived Bradley. "Uploading now."

CHAPTER 17

WHERE'S A GIANT METEOROID WHEN YOU NEED ONE?

Did you scare wickle Rafey?" Bradley said in a singsong voice as he scooped the python from my bed.

Sheila was so big it took all of Bradley's strength to lift the disgusting thing. "I wondered where you'd gone."

"Like you didn't know," I said.

"Rafe!" Mom cut in before Bradley could reply. She put an arm around my shoulders. "Don't be silly, honey. You'd have to be crazy to put a python in someone's bed."

"Well…," I muttered, but Mom didn't hear me. Perhaps it was for the best. She is usually someone who has my back, but she has this thing about being nice to people when you're staying in their home. In her book, being rude to a host is a big no-no.

"Sheila wouldn't hurt a fly, Ralph," Biff said as the snake draped herself around Bradley's shoulders and closed her eyes. "She's one of the family."

"Oh, yeah?" I sneered. "I'm not a fly, and the name's *Rafe,* not Ralph. Got it, you overgrown Ken doll?"

Or that's what I *would* have said if I had a spine.

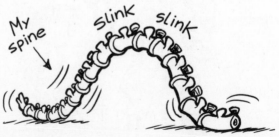

Instead, I just kind of grunted and stared at the floor, wondering when this would be over. I'd used up most of my dignity already, and winning an argument with someone whose TV you've just destroyed is always going to be difficult. Plus, Biff probably hadn't gotten over getting puked on by my mom yet.

Also, I was still only wearing my yellow boxer shorts. It's hard to get angry when all that stands between you and public nudity is a piece of thin cotton decorated with purple stars.

"Awesome!" Danny held up his phone. "Seven hundred and fifty-five hits in three minutes. Man, this clip is clocking up some serious action!"

Everyone whooped.

Except me—and Mom, although I think I saw the beginnings of a smile around her mouth.

She patted me on the head. "Go back to bed, sugar," she said quietly. "Try not to take it to heart. It'll all seem better in the morning."

I nodded even though I knew it wouldn't seem better in the morning. That was just the kind of thing that moms say. Mom meant well, but she hadn't looked deep into the shark eyes of the

Coogan twins. If those androids had anything to do with it, my life would be even worse in the morning. I skulked toward the stairs, turning around to face them when I heard them cackling like a bunch of monkeys in a laughing-gas factory.

Danny stopped howling long enough to hold up the screen of his phone toward me. "I uploaded the whole clip, man!" he yelled, tears rolling down his face. "You should check it out. It's on completefails.com. The clip's called 'Classic Rafe Khatcha*dork*ian All-Time Snake Fail.'"

"I wouldn't read the comments, dude," Belinda said, looking up from her own phone.

I knew Belinda wasn't trying to help me out. She was just letting me know that no matter how bad I thought the whole snake-screaming, TV-destroying humiliation had been, it was going to be a whole lot worse once everyone else on the planet had a chance to see it.

Gee, thanks, Belinda!

I turned around and went up the stairs to my room.

A while back, I'd seen a thing on TV about a giant meteoroid the size of Wyoming being on a possible collision course with Earth. If it hit, we'd all be wiped out in a split second.

Through the window, I looked up hopefully at the Shark's Bay night sky. Where was a giant meteoroid when you needed one?

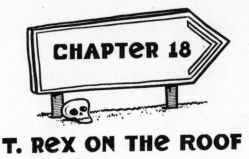

CHAPTER 18

T. REX ON THE ROOF

The next morning, it was like everything that had happened the previous night was a bad dream. Okay, it felt like I'd been rinsing my eyes with sand, my tongue had been replaced with what tasted like a dead rat, and I had cake crumbs wedged in areas I didn't know I had. But other than that, I felt pretty good.

Outside my window, the sun glinted on waves rolling onto a curving mile of gleaming white sand. Behind the beach, the town of Shark's Bay sparkled in the morning sun. The sky was blue and so was the crystal-clear water.

A pod of dolphins splashed in the surf. It was hot, but nothing like the cauldron of yesterday. Bright-green parrots screeched through the branches of trees that edged the shimmering backyard pool.

Other than Bradley and Belinda, who were swimming laps, the view was magnificent. *This trip might work out after all,* I thought.

"Not too shabby, eh?" Leo said, and I had to agree.

I could get used to this.

There wasn't even a trace of last night's storm. Other than a crane lifting a Tyrannosaurus rex off the roof of a house a couple of streets away.

"Back up there, cowboy," Leo said. "A *T. rex?*"

I jerked my head back toward the crane and saw that, despite no one in Shark's Bay seeming even slightly concerned, it actually was a T. rex being lifted off the roof.

And I was an expert on T. rexes. By which I mean that I'd seen all of the *Jurassic* movies and still had the purple plastic dinosaur that Grandma Dotty gave me when I was six. Like I said, an expert.

"Oh, come on," I muttered. "You gotta be kidding."

CHAPTER 19

BAD NEWS
AND MORE BAD NEWS

I was just about to open my mouth and yell "T. rex!" when my super Spidey sense kicked in, and I shut my mouth like a shark on a surfer's leg. Another split second and I would have started the day off by making a fool of myself *again*.

A T. rex in downtown Shark's Bay? Nuh-uh, don't think so. Not even *I* was dumb enough to think that Australia still had dinosaurs, no matter how ferocious and weird the rest of their animal population was.

So I squinted at the crane and took a closer look. The T. rex hung from the hook, its arms and legs sticking stiffly out of the large fabric sling wrapped around its belly. It was holding a sign for

Rex's Mightee Bites. So chances were pretty good it wasn't real.

I nodded and wiped my brow. That had been a close call. I didn't want to lose any more cool than I already had. After last night, I had very little reserves of cool left, and the last thing I needed to do was blow it all in a false T. rex panic.

my last can →

COOL

I got dressed and went downstairs. Mom was sitting on the pool deck drinking coffee with Biff and Barb Coogan.

"Morning, Rafe," Mom said, smiling. "Isn't this place great?"

"Uh-huh." It was the best I could do for now.

Mom seemed to have smoothed things over with Biff. She's good at that—smoothing things over, I mean. One of her many mom skills. Yesterday she'd hurled chunks all over Biff. Now, less than twenty-four hours later, she was chatting to him like nothing had happened. I couldn't imagine Belinda forgiving me that easily.

"You sssssssleep okay?" Biff asked. "Pillowssss sssssssoft enough?"

I smiled weakly.

Mom leaned over and squeezed my hand. "He's only joking, Rafe. Isn't that right, Biff?"

"Yessss," Biff said. "Sssssssorry, Rafe. I won't sssssssay another word about sssnakes."

He was telling the truth. He didn't say a *single* word about snakes. Instead, he said *lots* of words about snakes. After about fifteen minutes of lame snake jokes from Biff, I eventually managed to get some breakfast.

What is a snake's favorite school subject?

Hisstory!

What name do you give a snake in the grass?

Russell!

I really like deadly snakes—they've got poisonality!

"They'll get bored of all that snake stuff soon," Mom whispered to me. "Hang in there, honey. Today will be better, I promise."

"Okay," I said, and turned toward the table. I could use some better today.

Although, if the day was going to be an improvement upon yesterday, it didn't get off to a good start when Biff tried to make me eat something called Vegemite. The stuff looked like puréed dog poop. I opted for a bowl of Wheety Snax and a glass of juice instead.

"So," I said through a mouthful of flakes, "what's the plan today?"

I was looking forward to seeing a bit of Shark's Bay, maybe getting my toes wet at the beach (*just my toes*), and then taking a look at where I was supposed to be having my exhibition. Just thinking those words—*my exhibition*—gave me chills.

The first piece of bad news was that we wouldn't be going to the exhibition space just yet.

"They're still painting the place, Rafe," Biff said. "Should be finished by tomorrow."

Before I could say anything, Bradley and

Belinda walked up to the table, dripping in pool water and drying their cool surf hair with cool surf towels. Their eyes shot cool surf daggers at me.

We exchanged nods, and Belinda leaned toward Bradley and whispered something. Both of them looked back at me and started giggling. If you've ever had that happen to you, you'll know it feels about as reassuring as finding a bug in your burger.

Or a snake in your bed.

"So," Mom said, "me and Mr. and Mrs. Coogan are going to walk to the lighthouse. It was built in 1882! It's the first example of reflected electric light in this part of Australia."

I tried to look impressed. And failed.

"Great," I said.

Mom smiled. "I didn't think you'd go for that, so you're going with Bradley and Belinda and all their friends to the beach! Won't that be great?"

I spat my Wheety Snax across the table. I'm sure if Bradley and Belinda had been eating any, they'd have done the same.

That was the second chunk of bad news.

CHAPTER 20

THE SHORTS FROM HELL

Pretty much everyone in Shark's Bay was drop-dead gorgeous.

I found myself heading for the beach with Bradley and Belinda and their friends from last night, the ones who looked like they'd fallen right out of an Australian tourism ad. And then there was me, the poster boy for Awkwardsville.

To make matters worse, my online fame had spread faster than the bubonic plague. In the ten minutes it took to walk to the beach, three kids recognized me from completefails.com.

Just as we reached Bloodspurt Beach (I'm not kidding, that's what it's called), we passed some kids sitting in the shade of a tree who looked like they were in the wrong movie. For a start, none of them was particularly tall, particularly athletic, or particularly blond. They wore clothes that weren't surf cool, and they all looked like they'd just sucked on a slice of lemon.

I liked them immediately.

"Look at those sad sacks cluttering up the beach," Belinda said. "Total drongos."

I didn't know what a drongo was, but it sounded bad.

I was probably a drongo.

"The Outsiders," Bradley said. He growled at one of the boys in the group under the tree, who jumped back nervously. Bradley and his friends burst out laughing.

A dark-haired girl wearing black-rimmed glasses scowled at me.

I made a gesture that was meant to say, *Hey, sorry about all that, but I'm not really one of these cool surf types at all. I'm more of an artsy, TrollQuest-playing sort of guy, and I'm sure we could be friends if you'd only give it a shot.* But it's hard to get all that into one movement. I ended up looking like I was practicing the best way to crack open a coconut.

I wanted to hang with the Outsiders. They seemed much cooler than Bradley and Belinda's stupid buddies. They also had a cool name, even if they hadn't picked it for themselves. But from the icy expression on the dark-haired girl's face, it was clear that any "friend" of Bradley and Belinda's was most definitely *not* a friend of theirs. They hated me.

And my shorts.

THE SHORTS FROM HELL

Coincidentally, I should probably explain the shorts. Remember how Aussie Airways lost our bags? That meant I had to borrow a pair of swim trunks from Bradley. And Bradley gave me these monstrosities. He must have been keeping them as a practical joke.

For starters, they were about six sizes too big. More *longs* than shorts. They could have doubled as a tent. If the wind picked up to anything above a gentle breeze, I would be hoisted into the air like an empty plastic bag. My winter-pale Hills Village legs poked out from the bottom of them like a couple of bendy straws. And they had the *nastiest* pattern ever produced by humans—psychedelic Day-Glo butterflies, rainbows, hearts, and more puky stuff like that. These shorts were so bright you could probably see them from space.

I guess it could've been worse. I wasn't planning on going into the water, anyway.

Hey! Check out that kid's shorts!

With a sigh, I turned away from the Outsiders and trudged after the pod people toward Bloodspurt Beach. And it was only downhill from there.

CHAPTER 21

LET'S GO SURFING

Things went something like this:

1. Bradley and his crew picked up their surfboards and headed for the shark-infested water.
2. I really did not want to go into that water. There was a reason this town was called Shark's Bay, right?
3. I didn't want to look like a bigger loser than I already was, so my plan was to say that I'd love to go surfing, but unfortunately I didn't have a surfboard.
4. They had a spare surfboard.
5. My plan completely backfired.

Hey, isn't that snake-fail boy?

I tried to whip up some courage as we walked to the water's edge with our boards. I mean, I'd seen surfers on TV. How hard could it be? I could

swim and I could skateboard, and surfing was really just skateboarding on water, right? *I might even be really good at it,* I thought.

Plus, if I *was* really good at it, I might even conquer the Beast. And Bradley and Belinda and all the other cool surf types would gather around the beach bonfire to hear me talk about taming the monster wave. It might turn out to be the best thing I'd ever done!

It wasn't.

CHAPTER 22

A FREAKIN' HUGE SHARK

Attention! This is a Rafe Khatchadorian Public Health Warning!

Don't be like me. Don't listen to the voices in your head that tell you things will turn out okay. They won't. Above all, don't be dumb enough to go surfing. Trust me, it will end badly. Very badly.

This is because surfing absolutely *sucks*.

1. SURFING SUCKS SO MUCH THAT YOU COULD STICK A HOSE ON IT AND VACUUM YOUR WHOLE HOUSE IN SIX SECONDS FLAT.
2. SURFING SUCKS SO MUCH IT COULD DOUBLE AS A BLACK HOLE.
3. SURFING IS THE LITERAL DEFINITION OF SUCKOSITY.
4. AND SURFING IN AUSTRALIA IS THE SUCKIEST OF ALL BECAUSE THERE ARE SO MANY DIFFERENT WAYS TO GET MAIMED, INJURED, DROWNED, GOUGED, MOCKED, GRAZED, SLICED, DICED, AND ICED.

Listen and learn from my mistakes.

This is what surfing is really like.

The first thing I noticed was that the waves were much bigger close-up than they looked from the shore.

They were, in fact, ginormous.

The second problem was that getting a massive wall of plastic (a.k.a. the surfboard) past the huge breaker waves was almost impossible.

To make matters worse, the thing was strapped to my leg with a rope, so the board would snap back and smack into my head over and over again.

And by the time I did eventually scramble my way past the crashing white foam, I was a total wreck. I worked so hard to get to that point that I swear my eyeballs were sweating. *My eyeballs!* I didn't even know eyeballs *could* sweat.

And all of those problems were accompanied by another, bigger fear—sharks.

The entire time I was getting knocked around by the waves and gulping down lungfuls of salt water, there was the constant terror that somewhere beneath me was a FREAKIN' HUGE SHARK.

I swear I could hear the theme from *Jaws* playing over the sound of the waves.

Whatever huge monstrosity was down there could probably throw me up in the air like it was

tossing a marshmallow. At the top of my arc I would, just for a second, hang in the air above the beast—did I mention it was HUGE?—and see people on the beach running around like ants, screaming and panicking like you would if you'd just seen a FREAKIN' HUGE SHARK.

And then I'd be falling down, down, down, right into its gaping red maw.

Of course, since I'm still here writing this, you've probably already guessed that I didn't get eaten by a FREAKIN' HUGE SHARK. But surfing that morning on Bloodspurt Beach was, hands down, the worst hour of my life—worse than getting beat up by Miller the Killer before our truce. Worse than getting expelled. Worse than the worst thing you can think of times six. I think I swallowed about 8 percent of the Pacific Ocean. It was like being trapped inside a giant washing machine set to Spin. The ocean played with my rag-doll body for an hour and then spat me ashore like a gorilla spitting out an orange seed.

After all that, you'd think I'd be grateful to be back on dry land, and I would have been, except that when I did finally get back to the beach, I was *unconscious*.

As it turns out, *that* was the least of my problems.

CHAPTER 23

THE NAKED TRUTH

Being shredded by a massive wave after spending an hour in heavy surf is not recommended. I would have kicked the bucket for sure if it hadn't been for the dark-haired girl from the Outsiders.

When my skinny, surf-bashed body washed up into the shallows (I found out later), she sprinted across the sand, turned me over, and started giving me mouth-to-mouth.

That was when I woke up and thanked my rescuer by coughing a lungful of Pacific Ocean all over her.

(Side note: What is it with us Khatchadorians? We just can't stop puking on Australians!)

My name is Rafe, and I am a Pukeaholic. I haven't Puked on anyone for three days.

The dark-haired girl jumped to her feet, spattered with Khatchadorian lung drool. Then she turned on her heel and stalked back toward the trees, which was understandable.

I sat up. "Wait!" I yelled, or at least I would have if my lungs hadn't been filled with another sixty-eight gallons of salt water. I coughed up another bucketload, then heaved myself up and ran after her. "Wait up!" I yelled.

I ran right through the busiest part of the beach, and as I ran, I began to notice a strange sound getting louder and louder. My ears were full of water, so I ignored it and pursued my rescuer.

When the dark-haired girl reached the tree, she glanced back and, spotting me, put her hand to her mouth in shock. At that same moment, the water blocking my ears was dislodged and sound rushed in.

The first thing I heard was laughter—lots of it. And a few screams.

I glanced around. About eleven billion Australians were standing up, pointing at me, and laughing.

I mean, I knew I wasn't the best surfer ever, but this reaction was a bit over-the-top. I almost drowned! And my swim trunks weren't *that* ridiculous, were they? I glanced down at them to check for myself and realized instantly why the good people of Shark's Bay were laughing.

My psychedelic, Day-Glo, see-them-from-space shorts had been ripped to shreds, and I'd left the last shred on the beach when I started running. I was completely, absolutely, totally naked.

CHAPTER 24

CAN YOU BUY RADIOACTIVE SHARKS ONLINE?

You are proving to be very troublesome, Coogan."

I sat back in my white leather swivel chair ($952 from EvilGeniusFurniture.com) and stroked Mr. Meow's fluffy white fur. Mr. Meow purred softly and stared at the prisoner with his bright-green eyes.

"You have embarrassed me, and *that* I simply cannot allow." I pointed to the sharks in the pit. "Take a look at my little pets. They are very fine creatures, no? Their teeth have been specially sharpened by my assistant."

"Look," Bradley whined, "whoever you are, I'm sorry!"

"My name is Rafe Khatchadorian. You killed my father. Prepare to die!"

"I didn't kill your father!"

"No? Oh, wait, that's from a different movie," I said. "But you are still going to die."

"Please, Dr. Khatchadorian," Bradley begged. "I'm so, so sorry! It won't happen again, I swear!"

"Oh, you are right about that, Coogan." I smirked. "It will never happen again."

I leaned forward and pressed a button to release the prisoner's heavy chains.

"NOOOOOOOO!" Bradley screamed as he disappeared below the boiling surface of the water.

"Let that be a lesson to all enemies of Dr. Khatchadorian!" I cackled.

I would have made a great evil genius. No, really, I would have.

Unfortunately, I didn't have a secret lair or a pit of radioactive sharks. I didn't even have a cat, let alone a fluffy white one.

I would have to think of another way to exact my revenge.

After my swim trunk mishap, a woman at Bloodspurt Beach gave me a towel to cover up. But I still had to walk back through the laughing crowds, my face as red as a sunset on Mars. It was the longest walk of my life.

After getting all cleaned up and dressed, I sat by the Coogans' pool in the shade of a pandanus tree and thought dark, dark thoughts of vengeance.

Bradley Coogan would pay. Mark my words.

CHAPTER 25

KELL-ING ME SOFTLY

It turned out that wanting revenge was a lot easier than planning revenge. I was coming up blank on ideas for payback. After almost two hours of sulking by the pool, all I had to show for my efforts was a sunburned neck and a fat white splat of bird poop from a lorikeet on my shoulder. I didn't even try to wipe off the poop—that's how miserable I was.

Around three o'clock, Mom came back with Biff and Barb Coogan and a tall, tanned man wearing a khaki shirt, mirrored sunglasses, and shorts that were a little *too* short.

Short-shorts guy and Mom were laughing about something. My super Spidey senses went into overdrive instantly.

"Hi, Rafe," Mom sang. She looked happy.

I didn't like it.

I mean, I want my mom to be happy and everything, but there was something about short-shorts guy that put me on edge.

"Did you have a good time at the beach?" Mom asked.

"Of course he did!" Short-Shorts said before I could reply. "Who wouldn't have a good time on a ripper of a day like this? Catch any waves, grommet?"

Then he bent down and *ruffled my hair*. My hair hadn't been ruffled since I was in kindergarten, and I didn't like it back then, either.

"Oh, it was great," I said. "Apart from Bradley trying to drown me, and me ending up naked in the middle of the beach."

RUFFLE

"Oh, dear," Mom said, suddenly concerned. "That must have been awful, Rafe."

"That's right," Short-Shorts said. "Awfully funny!"

"I don't see how," I said in the coldest voice I could manage.

"No need to get your undies in a knot, mate," Short-Shorts said. "You need to lighten up a bit. Take that frown and put it upside down!"

Suddenly my idea about feeding someone to radioactive sharks sounded really good again.

"This is Kell," Mom said. "He's a friend of Biff and Barb's. Kell's a geologist who works for a big mining company."

I shrugged.

"Be nice, Rafe," she warned, giving me a look. "I'll let you two get to know each other." Mom headed back into the house with Biff and Barb.

Kell put out a hand the size of a bulldozer scoop. I could see myself reflected in his sunglasses. "Kell Weathers," he said. "Pleased to meet you, little man."

I let the "little man" comment slide and put my hand out reluctantly. "Rafe."

Kell gripped my hand and shook. I may as well have shoved my hand into a garbage disposal.

As much as I'd like to say that he went back to whatever rock he'd crawled out from under, Kell turned on his heel and walked into the Coogans' house to join Mom. He was clearly here to stay. But anyway, there'll be more on Kell later.

CHAPTER 26

THE ARTIST HAS LANDED

I didn't see much of the twins over the next couple of days, which was just fine by me. Belinda did snarkily mention that my snake video was up to 387,765 hits, and Bradley poured salt in my Wheety Snax once, but other than that, they left me to do my own thing.

Part of which involved going with Biff and Mom to see the Shark's Bay Surf Club, where my artwork was going to be exhibited in the brand-new clubhouse's lobby.

"Not bad, hey?" Biff said.

I had to admit it was pretty cool. Actually, the place was way cooler than I had imagined.

They'd built an indoor waterfall right at the entrance to the lobby. A cascade of water poured down a rock wall into a great big pool. There were blue and green lights under the water, which made the whole thing shimmer. It looked amazing. I couldn't imagine *anything* I produced being half as nice as this.

"Your artwork will be center stage, wRafe," Biff said. "Just to the left of the waterfall."

Mom beamed. "It's going to be fantastic!"

I suddenly felt really queasy and guilty.

"I haven't even started yet," I said.

Mom put her arm around my shoulders. "Whatever you do will be fantastic, honey."

"You'll be a knockout," Biff said. "We're all looking forward to seeing the great artist at work!"

In between all the visits to the beach, being naked in public, and devising ways to punish the twins of terror, I completely forgot the whole reason I was here. I hadn't even begun to think about what kind of art I'd be creating for my show. I gulped and wandered around the shiny new lobby, trying to look like I knew what I was doing.

I decided to take some photos of the space. I didn't have a clue yet what I was going to do, but I hoped the photos would give me some ideas.

Coming up with ideas always makes me have to go. The bathrooms hadn't been finished yet in the new clubhouse, so Biff pointed to a row of big gray boxes lined up on the lawn outside of the surf club entrance.

"Temporary dunnies," Biff said. He explained that *dunny* was the Australian word for *toilet*.

When I came back, Biff brought us to a place where I could work—a big, fully stocked room in the art department at Shark's Bay College. The place had everything I could possibly need to make something special, which, considering I had ABSOLUTELY NO IDEA what to fill the exhibition space with, made me even more nervous than I already was.

CHAPTER 27

THE OUTSIDERS

Later that day, I decided to skate back down to the college to see if I could find some artistic inspiration. I grabbed Bradley's best board from his room—one he'd told me never to touch, but whatever—and headed out.

I was rounding a bend at the bottom of a hill when I smacked straight into another skater. It was the dark-haired girl from the beach! I'd never gotten the chance to thank her, but then again, I'd been naked. Now that I had some clothes on, I could finally do it.

I helped her up and apologized. "Hi, I'm Rafe. I just wanted to say thanks. For, you know, saving my life."

"Oh, you," she said. "The artist."

I blinked. Me? And then I realized I *was* the artist. "How do you know who I am?" I asked.

She cocked her head. "Are you kidding? Everyone in town is talking about the crazy American nudist artist who has his own Complete Fails video." She stuck out her hand. "Ellie's the name."

The usual Khatchadorian conversation style

We shook hands, and for once, Rafe Khatchadorian actually managed to say the right thing to a girl.

"Would you like a smoothie?" I asked. It wasn't the best pickup line ever, but she did say yes, so I must have done something right.

There's a first time for everything.

We skated across to the T. rex burger joint, where the dinosaur was back in his rightful place. He certainly looked happy to be there again.

"On me," I said, pushing Ellie's mango smoothie across the table

139

when it arrived. "For being so good at mouth-to-mouth resuscitation."

I don't know what was smoother, me or what was in the glass.

Ellie put a finger in her mouth and pretended she was puking. "Puh-lease," she said. "Can't you see I'm eating? Or drinking? Do you eat or drink a smoothie?"

We talked for a while. Ellie told me all about growing up right here in Shark's Bay and how she'd always felt like she didn't belong. The rest of her friends were kind of the same, which is how they ended up hanging out together.

I admit I was a little jealous. I wished I had my own group of misfits back home. All I had was Flip. And Junior, but he's a dog.

"You know," Ellie said, "I thought you were one of the Coogan bozos when I first saw you heading out into the surf."

I shook my head. "I had no idea what I was doing."

"The Coogans should have known better," Ellie said. "It's *dangerous* out there." She paused and looked straight into my soul with her special truth-seeking laser-beam eyes. (Did I mention she had eyes like lasers? No? Well, she did.) "Unless you were dumb enough to *pretend* you could surf?"

"Um." I looked down at the table. My voice got real small. "I might have, sort of, kinda said I could..."

Ellie shook her head. "I thought so. Even the Coogans wouldn't send a newbie out there. And for them, the surf's not such a big deal. They like to think of themselves as the bravest family in town. Nothing scares Bradley Coogan—except frogs. He was in my biology class last year and kind of freaked out when a frog got loose."

"Frogs, huh?" I said.

A tickle of a whisper of a possibility popped into my mind, but I decided to leave it for now. The Big Revenge Plan could wait. I was enjoying myself for the first time since I arrived in Australia.

I slurped my smoothie. "Your friends and Bradley's friends don't get along, right?"

Ellie nodded. "You could say that. Bradley and the other morons dubbed us the Outsiders as an insult, but we kind of like it, so that's what we call ourselves now. We're just into different things than them. That beach stuff isn't really our idea of fun. I mean, a couple of the guys surf, but it's not our thing."

"So what is your thing?" I asked.

"Movies," Ellie said, her eyes lighting up. "We make horror movies."

I didn't see that one coming, but as soon as Ellie said the words, I had a lightbulb moment. I leaned closer. "Tell me more."

CHAPTER 28

A DROP BEAR ATE MY SANGA

Kell Weathers dangled helplessly at the end of my arm. He'd made the mistake of trying his old hand-crushing handshake routine for the last time, and now he would regret it.

What Weathers didn't realize was that I'd signed up as a NASA test subject for experimental android technology, and I was about to get my revenge.

"Would you like a sausage sandwich or some barbecued ribs?" Kell said.

Considering the situation, it seemed like a funny thing for him to say.

"Rafe?" Kell said again. "Sausage sanga? Drink?"

I suddenly blinked and saw Mom looking at me

strangely. I had fallen asleep on a lounge chair on the Coogans' pool deck, right in the middle of the party.

"What?" I said.

"You were miles away," Mom said. She put her hand across my forehead in the way that moms do.

"I wish I were miles away," I mumbled.

"Play nice," Mom said. "For me?"

I sighed and nodded.

Mom was right. She was enjoying her trip to Australia, and I didn't want to spoil things for her, even if she did have a blind spot when it came to tan Australian geologists. The sky was blue, the sun was shining, and I was about to dig into a plate of ribs. What did I have to complain about?

Especially since I was meeting Ellie and the rest of the Outsiders at the movies later. With *that* to look forward to, I could manage the next few hours.

Although, as Mom wandered over to Kell Weathers at the grill, I felt the fingers of my right hand twitch. A robotic steel claw could definitely come in handy.

THE TINGLE

I stretched and yawned, then got up to go do my Mom-pleasing duty. The place was packed with the people of Shark's Bay. When Mom reached up to touch Kell's shoulder, he looked in my direction and smiled threateningly. I got that super Spidey tingle all over again. I'd have to watch this situation closely.

The party wasn't as bad as I thought it would be. At one point Biff dragged me around like some sort of trophy and introduced me as "the American artist." Surprisingly, people seemed to be pretty interested about me winning the prize, so I relaxed and tried to enjoy myself. After an hour of small talk and smiling so much my jaw ached, I grabbed some food and my sketchbook and found a quiet spot under the trees by the pool. I had just taken a bite of my grilled cheese sandwich when Kell appeared, holding a can of soda.

"Thought you looked a bit thirsty there, Rafey," he said, passing me the can. The soda was ice cold.

147

I looked at it suspiciously.

"Look," Kell continued, "I know we haven't exactly hit it off, but I'm really not a bad guy, and I couldn't let you sit around over here without giving you a heads-up, you being from overseas and everything."

"A heads-up?"

Kell pointed at the branches above my head. "It's highly unlikely, but we do have a small problem in Australia: drop bears. You heard of 'em?"

Drop bear

A chill ran down my back.

"There are drop bears here?" I asked, looking up at the trees nervously.

Kell nodded. "They can smell fresh meat in the neighborhood." He eyed my sandwich. "And they do love a cheese sanga. Watch yourself, mate."

I looked at Kell. Maybe I'd been wrong about him. Perhaps he wasn't so bad after all.

"Thanks," I said, and opened the can.

As I did, two things happened.

The first was that the soda exploded all over my face, temporarily blinding me.

The second (and this one was much more worrying) was that I felt something furry fall onto my head and wrap its arms around my neck.

A drop bear!

I screamed like a startled pony and leaped backward. For a split second, my feet teetered on the edge of the pool, and then, with an almighty splash, I fell in, clawing wildly at the drop bear on my head. I wasted no time in expertly sucking in about eighty-three gallons of chlorinated water and sank below the surface, sure that at any moment the thing was going to rip open the top of my skull and commence drop bear dinner. Main course: Khatchadorian brain à la mode.

I erupted from the pool like a ballistic missile shooting from a submarine, dragging the creature off my neck. Without hanging around to see what happened to the drop bear, I kicked toward the edge of the pool so fast it was like someone had strapped a speedboat engine onto my rear end and pressed the Start button.

Surrounded by a foam of white water (caused

by my high-speed arm flailing), I wondered why no one was diving in to save me. Couldn't they see that I was about to be eaten alive? Or maybe they were too scared of the drop bear?

And then I saw the pool was surrounded by laughing faces.

I got an awful feeling of déjà vu.

I stopped swimming and looked around. A stuffed animal—a pink bear—bobbed on the surface of the pool. I looked up and glimpsed Bradley in the branches of a nearby tree, laughing like he'd just swallowed a joke book.

The whole dirty trick became as clear as the Coogans' swimming pool.

I'd been tricked. In public. *Again.*

I clambered out of the pool with as much dignity as I could. Which, in case you were wondering, was exactly zero.

"C'mon, Rafey," Kell shouted as I stalked toward the house. "It's only a joke, mate!"

I said nothing, but one thing was certain. Kell Weathers had just joined Bradley Coogan at the very, very top of the Rafe Khatchadorian Revenge List.

CHAPTER 29

YOU WON'T LIKE ME WHEN I'M ANGRY

It was horrible.

Bloodshot eyes, a gaping mouth full of broken yellow teeth, and flaking gray skin. I felt my breathing becoming panicky as the thing reached out toward me, its decaying hands getting closer and closer and…

I whipped off my 3-D glasses and sank back into my seat as the zombies swam out of focus. I sneaked a quick glance at Ellie to see if she'd noticed how badly I had just freaked out over seeing that flesh-eater come right toward us.

She had.

"Are you okay?" she whispered.

I rubbed the bridge of my nose. "Um, these glasses give me a headache."

"Uh-huh." Ellie's smile made me suspect she didn't believe me, but she returned her gaze to the screen without saying anything else.

I left the glasses off and watched the rest of *Zombies Ate My Brain* in a red-and-blue haze. Just before the movie ended, I put the 3-D glasses back on so the rest of the Outsiders wouldn't think I was a total wimp.

Afterward, we all got slushies in the movie theater café and discussed the finer points of zombie etiquette.

The Outsiders knew *a lot* about zombies.

Now would probably be a good time to introduce them.

Dingbat Ellie Mikey Sal Nico

The Outsiders knew a lot about horror movies, period. I was impressed and got a whole lot more impressed when I found out that Ellie was the Outsider in charge of special effects.

"She's good," Nico said. "Ellie knows her stuff."

The rest of the Outsiders nodded.

"You should see her latest monster," Nico said. "It's a beaut."

"It's a bunyip," Sal added. She was the smallest of the Outsiders and was almost hidden behind her slushy.

"A *what?*" I said.

"*Revenge of the Teenage Zombie Bunyip from*

Mars," Ellie said. "That's our new movie. Bunyips are these weird sort of giant amphibians."

"I've never heard of them," I said.

"They're pretty much strictly an Aussie thing," Ellie said. She sounded sort of proud. "Like frogs, but bigger and angrier."

My ears pricked up at the mention of frogs. Where had I heard about them recently?

Oh, right…Bradley was pee-his-pants scared of them.

And—*BING!*—just like that, a magnificently evil plan began to form in my brain. A plan for revenge. A plan so monstrous that it would probably lead to the collapse of civilization—or at least the part of civilization that included Shark's Bay.

The only question was, would I be willing to risk everything, including my mom's wrath, to get even with Bradley?

I was still thinking about it when Ellie pulled me to the side.

"What's up?" I said.

She frowned. "You haven't seen it?"

"Seen what?"

Ellie held out her phone and pressed the Play button on a video clip. It was only a short piece of footage—me screaming and falling into the Coogans' pool. The clip had racked up basically a trillion hits already.

I hadn't mentioned the whole drop bear incident to Ellie yet, so I tried to play it cool. If you can call having your face catch on fire in the middle of the theater café cool. Okay, so I didn't *actually* play it cool. I was mad. I was *seething*.

"Are you all right?" Ellie asked.

"NYAAAAARGGGH!" I roared as I started to swell up and turn green right there in the middle of the café. My eyes glowed fiery red, and muscles I didn't know I had bulged from my arms. I ripped open my shirt, flexed my giant green biceps, and roared like a wounded lion. I lifted a fist the size of a basketball and smashed a life-size cutout of Leonardo DiCaprio into smithereens. As people started screaming and running in all directions,

I stamped my big green foot down. The ground shook. I—

"Rafe!" Ellie yelled. "I said, are you all right?"

I blinked and looked down at my skinny nongreen arm. "Sorry, I spaced out." I laced my fingers together and cracked my knuckles. "This bunyip of yours," I said to Ellie, "can I see it?"

CHAPTER 30

SELFISH? ME?

The next day I had to wait for Ellie to get home from school before I could go and see the bunyip.

The hours crawled past. The Coogans were out at work, Bradley and Belinda were back in school, and Mom had gone off somewhere with my archenemy, Kell Weathers. What with Bradley and Belinda and Kell, not to mention the rest of the Surf Gorillas, that list of sworn enemies was getting longer than one of Georgia's school supply lists. And that's without bringing up all of the sworn enemies I had back in the US.

Of all my rivals, though, Kell was the one who worried me most. I wanted revenge on Bradley, but Kell's friendship with Mom was a teeny-tiny concern.

Leo, who had been keeping a low profile recently, passed me a drawing.

"Very funny," I said. But maybe Leo was right. Perhaps I *was* being shellfish—I mean selfish. Maybe Mom *deserved* some attention, even if it was from a hand-crushing creep like Kell.

Reluctantly, I crossed Weathers off my list of enemies. We'd never be what you might call buddies, but I didn't need to let my dislike of him spoil Mom's trip. I felt a warm glow inside, and it wasn't because I'd accidentally swallowed a chili. I felt *noble*.

When it was time for me and my halo to go to Ellie's place, I grabbed Bradley's prized skateboard and zipped there as fast as I could go.

It was a hot day and the thunderclouds had been building for hours. As I reached Ellie's street, the first fat raindrops began to fall and I heard the distant rumble of thunder.

Ellie lived a few blocks back from the beach in a less swanky part of Shark's Bay, where the houses were made of timber and stood on stilts. Lots of them had small boats in the yard or old cars that were being fixed up. The streets were lined with shady trees, and the whole place was a lot funkier than down by the shore. It felt more like where I came from. I liked it.

I hoped this bunyip of Ellie's matched my vision of it. My whole plan depended on it looking like a monstrous demon frog from Bradley's worst nightmares.

I walked up to her door and knocked.

No pressure.

CHAPTER 31

I WAS WORKING IN THE LAB LATE ONE NIGHT...

Hi," Ellie said when she opened the door.

"I'm here," I announced, smiling.

"I can see that, Einstein," Ellie said. "And stop smiling like that. It makes you look like a nut." She turned and walked back into the house. "Follow me. My dad's still at work."

I almost asked where her mom was, when I remembered Nico mentioning that Ellie's mom died when she was little. *That would've been great, Khatchadorian,* I said to myself. Real tactful. I reached up and adjusted my imaginary halo.

Ellie's house seemed normal—not too tidy, with a TV, kitchen, furniture. A bit boring. But downstairs, things were different. *Very* different.

"My dad put in walls between the stilts to make this into a basement," Ellie explained. "It might be a problem if the place ever gets flooded again, but we'll deal with that when it happens. Until then, this is my workshop!"

I couldn't speak. Ellie's workshop was the coolest place I'd ever seen. The walls were lined with shelves of paint, tools, bits of models, plastic horror masks, electronics, lights, rolls of canvas, paper, pieces of wood, coils of wire, spray cans, cleaning fluids, remote-controlled devices, mirrors—anything that looked like it might be useful for making an animatronic bunyip was there.

A massive, paint-spattered table stretched the length of Ellie's workshop. Lying in the center was something under a white sheet. A spaghetti mess of wires snaked out from under the sheet onto the floor of the basement. A vise on a nearby table held what looked like an alien arm.

Ellie pulled back the sheet. "There it is."

Thunder cracked outside, and lightning cast shadows that flickered across the walls. Lying flat on its back, missing an arm and looking exactly like it was asleep, was Ellie's bunyip.

It was *gigantic*.

It was **terrifying**.

It was ***perfect***.

"Wow," I said.

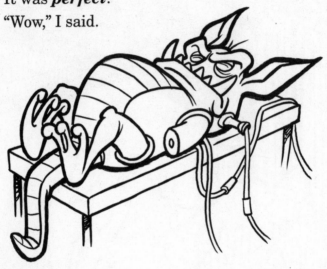

The bunyip really was *wow*. It was as *wow* as anything I'd ever seen. It frightened *me* half to death, and I knew it was just a bundle of rubber and electronics.

"That is amazing. Does it move?" I asked.

Ellie picked up a remote control from the workbench and pressed a switch. There was a soft electronic hum, and then the bunyip's eyes opened slowly and glowed red. Ellie turned a dial on the remote and the bunyip sat up on the bench. It swung its head in my direction and howled so loudly I could feel the bass shaking my spine.

"One hundred and forty-three decibels," Ellie said proudly. "Twin-mounted deep-bass equalized speakers with double woofers and a Swiss-made magnifying reverberator."

I didn't understand a word she said, but I knew one thing: Ellie's bunyip was going to make all my dreams come true.

"I've got a plan," I said. I didn't mean to say anything, but seeing the bunyip made the words just come rushing out. *Ivegotaplan.* Blurp! Just like that.

"Plan for what?" Ellie said.

I shook my head. "Forget I said anything."

Ellie tilted her head to one side and looked at me, her lips pursed. "Is this about getting revenge on Bradley and Belinda?"

I don't know if Ellie was some sort of mind reader or what—for all I knew, she could be a star graduate from the Zurich Institute of Psychic Talents—but she had read *my* thoughts as clearly as a billboard.

"Is it that obvious?"

Ellie nodded.

"So…?"

Ellie didn't say anything for about a hundred years.

"I'll think about it," she said eventually. "You're going back to Hills Village, but I have to live here with them every day. And I'm guessing this plan might involve my bunyip, right? I put a lot of work into that thing."

I nodded. Ellie was contemplating helping me out with my plan, and that's all I could ask for.

It was a start.

CHAPTER 32

THE PLAN: DAY ONE

My mission, should I choose to accept it—and I had choosed—was to get into the Shark's Bay Surf Club, covertly take measurements, and get out, all while staying alive, if possible.

I braced myself against the edge of the skylight, hooked the titanium wire onto my belt, and adjusted my night-vision goggles. Below me, the raging torrent of the waterfall rushed past before falling almost six thousand miles to the boiling pool set into the floor of the lobby far, far below.

"Careful, Khatchadorian," Ivan Awfilitch, my mission controller, snarled into my earpiece. "You've only got one shot at this! If you mess up, HQ is going to bury you so deep they'll need a team of miners to find you."

"Check," I said.

I had my analog-level measuring device (a tape measure) in one hand and a state-of-the-art measurement-recording platform (a notebook) in the other. My image-retention device (a camera) was hanging around my neck.

I gave Ivan a final salute and dropped into the abyss, quickly lowering into the lobby at the end of the wire. One slip and I could get seriously splashed.

Down, down, down I slid until I reached a point just above the surface of the pool and stopped dead, perfectly balanced only inches from the water. The night-vision goggles identified the tracks of the surf club's security-system lasers and...

Well, that's what I would have done if I'd had to sneak into the club, anyway. In the end, I just walked up and went inside. (See why I had to spice it up a little?)

The lobby of the club was deserted, apart from a woman who looked like she might be the manager.

"Take your time, honey," she said. She pointed at a poster on the wall. "Have you sorted out your costume yet?"

"Costume?" I said.

The poster was advertising the grand opening. My name was up there and I experienced a little thrill seeing my name in print.

"Nobody mentioned a costume party," I said, but the manager had gone off to do whatever it is managers do.

173

I hadn't considered the possibility that this thing would have costume requirements. But then again, costumes seemed to be really important to Australian people. Biff had picked us up at the airport dressed as a chicken, after all. I guessed costume parties were another one of those mysterious Australian things, like cricket and Vegemite and wearing short shorts in public. It was also a complication I could do without, but as I considered it more carefully, I realized that a costume could come in handy.

I opened up my measurement-recording platform, unrolled my analog-level measuring device, and started taking down numbers. If we were going to get this right, we couldn't afford making a single mistake.

ACTION!

I'd never been on a film set before. To be honest, it wasn't as glamorous as I thought it would be, even if it was just the Outsiders filming *Revenge of the Teenage Zombie Bunyip from Mars*.

We were standing around on a patch of scrubby ground next to a sugarcane field a couple of miles west of Shark's Bay. The equipment they were using wasn't exactly high-tech. The Outsiders were shooting on anything they could get their hands on—camcorders, smartphones, even an ancient Super 8 camera that used actual film. But they still seemed to know what they were doing.

"We do most of the sound later," Nico explained. "There's usually too much background interference if we record it live."

They were filming a chase scene through the cane field and were having some trouble deciding how to do it. I suggested that we could sketch out a few ideas beforehand just to figure things out, and it seemed to work.

"Hey! You can be our storyboard artist," Ellie said.

Until then I didn't know there was such a thing as a storyboard artist. I'd never thought about my drawings being *useful* before.

My storyboard →

① Cane field – misty ... spooky

② close-up on Dingbat scared, lost ...

③ Dingbat's view: a "wall" of sugarcane.

④ Dingbat hears a sudden noise! Close-up.

CRACK!

⑤ Top of the sugarcane field. It's moving!

⑥ Dingbat runs!

I sat underneath the shady part of a tree and started sketching. *Maybe these drawings could be in the exhibit at the surf club,* I thought. I did need something to deflect attention from my evil plan, after all.

I still had to convince the Outsiders to help. They were no fans of Bradley and Belinda and the rest of the Surf Gorillas, but what I was planning needed some real motivation. The Outsiders hadn't been publicly humiliated like me.

That's three times.

As I sketched, I wondered if they would risk everything just to help me get revenge.

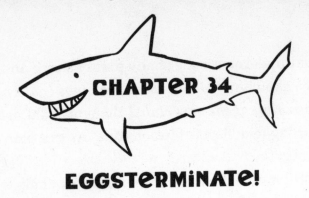

CHAPTER 34

EGGSTERMINATE!

The push that sent Ellie over the edge came sooner than I'd thought.

It was the last shot of the day and the most complicated. It was also the most expensive by a mile. Ellie and the rest of the Outsiders had saved up a whole bunch of money for it and managed to buy some fireworks from a movie-prop supplier in Sydney, rent a dry-ice machine to make fog, and prepare buckets of fake blood.

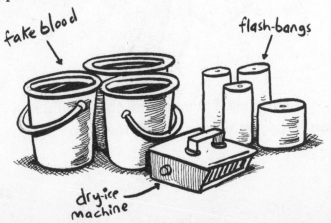

fake blood

flash-bangs

dry-ice machine

"This has got to go right the first time," Ellie said.

Nico, the director, gave instructions to Mikey and Dingbat, who were playing the two characters. It was up to Ellie to time the fireworks, turn on the dry-ice machine, and throw the buckets of blood. Nico had one camera—the best one—and they gave me a smartphone to film things from another angle, just as a backup. A third camcorder was propped up on a tree stump to film the scene as a long shot.

"Everyone ready?" Nico said. "Let's get this right, okay? We've got about three minutes of sunlight left!"

Ellie counted down the scene. "Three, two, one…"

"Action!" Nico yelled.

Ellie pressed the Start button on the dry-ice machine, and we began filming.

Mikey and Dingbat came out of the cane field right on cue, and Ellie started setting off the fireworks. They looked amazing. Ellie smiled and looked over at me. Grinning, I gave her a thumbs-up.

As Ellie threw the first of the buckets of fake blood over Dingbat, an egg exploded on the ground in front of her. She looked at it, puzzled, and then a second egg hit Mikey on the shoulder, followed by a bag of flour.

A shower of eggs and flour cascaded down on the set, and then crashing through the sugarcane came the Surf Gorillas, yelling and screaming. Before any of the Outsiders could react, they ran through the set, scattering script sheets to the wind and kicking over the buckets of blood.

"Losers!" Bradley shouted as they ran off, laughing and hooting.

"Film this, you geeks!" Belinda screeched.

The Outsiders stood and watched them go. The shot was ruined.

As the sky darkened, Ellie walked over to me. She had egg in her hair and an expression on her face that would not have looked out of place in a horror movie.

"This revenge plan of yours?" she said. "What do you need? I'm in."

CHAPTER 35

KELL GOES BARKING MAD

Life carried on as usual at the Coogans', which meant that Bradley and Belinda took every opportunity to remind me what a loser I was.

I didn't care. Much.

Let them think they'd gotten away with the Great Cane Field Ambush. Let them think I was too much of a wuss to get revenge. They'd find out soon enough that Rafe Khatchadorian was a force to be reckoned with.

As would Kell Weathers.

A force to be reckoned with →

Really?

Kell had let his true nature slip through his fake nice-guy act one night when he came over to pick up my mom for a date. She was busy getting ready upstairs when Kell walked up to me.

I'd been giving him the silent treatment the last couple of times I saw him. I still remembered his part in the Great Drop Bear Incident, and even though I wasn't going to try to get revenge on him, I wasn't ready to let bygones be bygones, either. Neither was he, apparently.

"You don't like me too much, do you, *Rafe?*" He prodded me in the chest. It hurt. I guess geologists have strong fingers from picking up all those rocks.

I shrugged, trying to ignore the pain. Then Kell jabbed me again.

"I asked you a question, *Rafey.*"

I shrugged once more, and right in front of my eyes, Kell began to mutate into a werewolf.

Hair sprouted from his face, and his hands curled into vicious-looking claws. His eyes glowed red, and drool dripped from between his fangs and slid down over his bottom lip. He looked a bit like

Hugh Jackman's less handsome Wolverine brother crossed with a rabid German shepherd.

"If I didn't like your mom so much, I'd clobber you," Kell the Werewolf hissed.

I didn't even know werewolves *could* hiss, which just goes to show that you learn something new every day.

"And if you mention a word of this to her, I'll deny it all." Kell threw back his head to howl at the moon. There wasn't a moon visible, so he howled at the lightbulb hanging from the ceiling.

I guess werewolves can't always get full-moon access.

By the time Mom came downstairs looking glitzy, Kell had lost all trace of his inner werewolf.

"Nice to see you two getting along," Mom said. She smiled so wide I didn't have the heart to tell her that her friend Kell was a chest-prodding bully. Plus a mutant werewolf.

"Best of mates," Kell said. He looked at me. "Isn't that right, Rafey?"

I nodded, not trusting myself to speak.

Mom and Kell headed out toward the bright lights of Shark's Bay, laughing and joking like two lovebirds. Seeing Mom all dressed up, I was struck with a horrible thought: *Kell Weathers is going to ask her to marry him tonight!*

No one wants a werewolf as a stepfather.
I mean, being *thisclose* to having a bear as a
stepfather a while ago was enough to scare me
pretty good. Besides, it wasn't so much Kell being
a drooling creature of the night that worried me,
although that would be pretty inconvenient. It was
him getting super friendly with my mom and what
that could mean for my family. The night before,
I was using Mom's laptop and noticed she'd been
reading up on Australia's immigration laws.

I had no real problem with Australians (other
than Bradley, Belinda, and the Surf Gorillas—and
Kell, of course), but I wasn't eager to
become one anytime soon. The
whole thing was starting to
make me depressed.

I went to my room,
rubbing the sore spot on
my chest, and sat down
on the bed. This was going
to require some serious
thought.

CHAPTER 36

TRUE GRIT

When Mom and Kell got back from their night out, Kell grabbed me "playfully" around the neck and began ruffling my hair.

I hate having my hair ruffled by someone I *like*. Having it done by a creep like Kell Weathers almost made me hurl.

"Ow!" I yelled, rubbing my scalp.

Mom sighed. "Kell's just being nice, Rafe."

"Don't blame the little feller, Jules," Kell said. "The kid just needs some grit."

"Oh, you want grit?" I yelled. "I'll give you grit!"

I leaped across the room, grabbed Kell around the neck, and threw him at the wall.

"Don't hurt me!" Kell squealed as he lay sprawled on the floor.

"Rafe, stop!" Mom yelled. "He's only a geologist!"

"Too late!" I shouted. "Rafe the Chafe takes no prisoners!"

I leaped from the top rope of the ring and slammed into Kell, hard. Wrapping my sandpapery arms around his head, I gave him the worst friction burn ever experienced on three continents. A grown man in the audience burst into tears. Sandpapering a man's head is just *nasty*, but I had been pushed to the limit, and I ruffled his hair even harder.

Oh, that's gotta hurt! Rafe "the Chafe" Khatchadorian looks like he's in a really scratchy mood tonight, folks!

"Oh, the humanity!" the commentator wailed.
"Won't the referee stop this madness? No one can
take this kind of punishment! The Geologist won't
have a head left if this goes on much longer!"

He was right. Within a minute, all that
remained of Kell's head was a pile of wood
shavings.

I got to my feet and the referee lifted my arm
in the air.

"And the winner is...Rafe! Rafe. Rafe. *RAFE?*"

I opened my eyes. Kell, his head far too intact for my liking, was leaning over me, my mom looking over his shoulder.

"You must have drifted off there for a minute, mate," Kell said. Then, with his back to my mom, he mouthed, "Wimp."

Yup. Kell Weathers was *definitely* at the top of the People Rafe Khatchadorian Hates List.

CHAPTER 37

LET'S GET THINGS STARTED

The next day, Ellie and I really got moving on Operation ROCK (Revenge on the Coogan Kids). With just over twenty-four hours to go before the big night at the surf club, there wasn't a moment to waste.

Ellie built a scale model of the surf club lobby out of cardboard, and we plotted out every step with the rest of the Outsiders.

"This has got to be perfect," I said, pacing the floor of Ellie's workshop. I pointed my pointy stick (everyone planning something like this needs a pointy stick) at the model. "And top secret. If word gets out to the Surf Gorillas, we're finished."

The Outsiders nodded solemnly. No one was going to snitch.

Nico and I went out to the club and cased the joint for the best time to get everything inside. We'd had a stroke of luck with our plans—it turned out Nico's older sister was the club manager I'd seen before.

"She keeps the key to the building in her purse," Nico said as we crouched in the bushes across the road from the club.

"Can you get a copy?" I asked.

Nico held up a key and smiled. "Way ahead of you, dude."

"Tonight?"

Nico nodded. "Tonight."

Operation ROCK was a go.

CHAPTER 38

THE POINT OF NO RETURN

It was the big night. We had done all we could. Everything was in place.

The sketches I'd done for the Outsiders' shoot were framed and placed on three easels on a small stage at one side of the waterfall. I called the drawings *Zombie Movie Sketches* because, well,

ZOMBIE MOVIE SKETCHES
artist: Rafe Khatchadorian, pencil on paper

they were sketches of the zombie movie. I'm clever like that. Biff had put up a big banner with the title, which hung over the easels. It made me feel pretty special.

Last night the Outsiders and I had broken about nineteen billion laws to set up what we needed inside the surf club. We didn't get much sleep, but we didn't care.

Tonight was payback time.

Ellie and I—she was dressed as Frankenstein's monster and I went as Igor—arrived around seven o'clock. As we neared the entrance, I could see through the windows that the place was already knee-deep in pirates and princesses, Elvises and Ewoks, superheroes, aliens, and ballerinas.

Bradley, with about as much imagination as a jellyfish in a coma, had gone as a 1970s surfer, and Belinda was a punk rocker. Kell was a werewolf—spooky, right?—and my mom had gone as what looked like Wonder Woman's second cousin.

Just outside the entrance, a gorilla was cooking sausages on a giant grill. As Ellie and I walked by, the gorilla removed his head to reveal a sweating Mayor Biff Coogan, who looked like he was beginning to regret his choice of costume. Maybe he should've stuck with the chicken suit, puke stink and all.

"The star of the show!" Biff said as he saw me. He waved a plate of sausage sandwiches at us. "Sausage sanga, Picasso?"

I felt my stomach lurch and shook my head. I was so nervous that I was sure anything I ate would come straight back up. "No, thanks," I said, and darted inside.

Before I knew what was happening, Mom grabbed me and pulled me toward a man dressed all in black with a gray beard. "This is Frost DeAndrews, the famous art critic," she said. "He's come all the way up from Sydney!"

"Hi," I said. "What's your costume?"

DeAndrews looked puzzled, then pursed his lips. "We don't *do* fancy dress in Sydney."

Frost DeAndrews

How to spot an art critic...

Sunken eyes

Hipster beard

Lemon-sucking lips

Black jacket

Heart of solid ice (not shown)

Hands in pockets to indicate total boredom with everything

Black jeans

General air of superiority

Uncomfortable shoes

"Oh," I said. "Okay."

"I'm so proud of you, Rafe. The drawings look great!" Mom gushed. "Don't they, Mr. DeAndrews?"

"Quite," DeAndrews said, bending his lips in what I imagined was meant to be a smile. He looked like he had something smelly right under his nose. "I'm sure the folks in Happy Valley would find them utterly delightful."

He leaned in a little closer toward me.

"Didn't you get time to finish them?" he whispered. He waved his hand at my drawings. "Frankly, from what Mayor Coogan told me, I was expecting a bit more than *doodles*. Drawings are so passé." Frost DeAndrews shuddered. "Maybe next time, dear boy, you should try some *ideas*— proper art. Hmm? Something that knocks my socks off. This whole trip is beginning to look like a complete waste of time."

This conversation clearly wasn't going too well. Before I said something I might have regretted, Biff Coogan's voice came over the speakers, welcoming everyone to the exhibition.

Just like his brother back in Hills Village, Biff Coogan liked the sound of his own voice. Next to me, Ellie checked her watch and then pulled me across to a quieter corner of the lobby.

"We'd better get into position," she said.

"You still think this is a good idea?" I whispered back.

"Why? Are you getting cold feet?" she said.

"No," I said, lying through my teeth. I was more nervous than a sackful of turkeys on Thanksgiving. Then I thought of Frost DeAndrews. If nothing else, he would see what I'd really made for the exhibition. I hoped he had good socks on, 'cause I was about to knock them off.

"Psst!" someone hissed close to my ear.

I turned to find myself looking at an asteroid.

A panel in the asteroid slid back to reveal Nico's face. "Ready?" he asked.

"An asteroid?" I said. "How do you go to the bathroom dressed like that?"

"Never mind that!" Nico said. "Are you ready?"

I was still curious about the asteroid costume and the toilet problem, but I didn't push it. Nico was right—we had bigger fish to fry.

"Mikey and Dingbat are on standby," Nico reported. "Are we a go?"

I took a deep breath and nodded. "Let's do it."

CHAPTER 39

GO! GO! GO!

Sal's job was to cut the lights. She was positioned near the stairwell leading to the basement, where the fuse box was located. I saw her looking over at me and Ellie and Nico behind the curtains, waiting for the final go-ahead, while Mayor Coogan droned on. Sal raised her eyebrows in a question.

I was about to give the thumbs-up to start things rolling when an image of Principal Stricker suddenly flashed into my mind.

I'd been given this trip to Australia as a gift from the towns of Hills Village and Shark's Bay. If we did this thing—if we followed through with Operation ROCK and everyone knew I'd caused so much trouble here—Principal Stricker would *not* be happy. Nobody would be happy—not Mom, not either of the mayors, not a single one of the good citizens of Shark's Bay other than the Outsiders.

But it was the thought of how Principal Stricker would react that sent a shiver of pure fear trickling down my spine. I could feel her disapproval vibrating all the way across the Pacific Ocean.

Beware the mighty power of Stricker...

At that moment, Ellie reached out and squeezed my hand. She must have known I was wavering. I don't know how, but she just did, and the quick touch of her hand gave me all the confidence I needed.

I gave Sal the thumbs-up. She nodded and ducked out of sight, down the stairwell. Stage one had begun.

"You ready?" Ellie said.

Before I could reply, all the lights went out in the lobby and we were plunged into blackness. There were a couple of jokey screams and a few people started laughing.

"Someone forgot to pay the power bill!" Kell shouted.

"At least it stopped the speeches!" someone else shouted.

"Initiate stage two," I whispered to Nico.

I heard some rustling in the dark as Nico fumbled for a switch hidden somewhere inside the asteroid costume. Nico was the Outsiders' expert on lighting and sets. Mikey and Dingbat were in their positions in the basement, making sure we had power.

From under the bubbling water in the pool at the foot of the waterfall, an eerie green light began to glow. A thin mist drifted up from its surface. Green shadows danced spookily across the walls, and the lobby grew strangely quiet. People began to cluster around the edge of the pool.

"Wow," I whispered. "That looks great!"

"I went for the zombie-apocalypse look," Nico replied.

"It's the end of the world!" Bradley yelled, but no one laughed.

"What on earth…?" I heard Biff Coogan say.

I saw Forest DeAndrew starting to look interested for the first time all evening. It was all the incentive I needed.

"Do it," I whispered to Ellie.

She picked up her remote control and thumbed the On switch, and we moved to stage three of Operation ROCK.

I ignored Principal Stricker's and the Hills Village mayor's imaginary voices expelling me from the middle school *and* the town. That's the great thing about imaginary people.

Besides, it was too late to stop now.

CHAPTER 40

FREAK OUT!

The surface of the pool erupted and Ellie's bunyip—eyes glowing red and mouth gaping wide to reveal a row of fearsome, razor-sharp choppers—came roaring up from the depths like a creature from your worst nightmare. Believe me, this one was an absolute doozy.

"AWOOOOAAARGH!" the bunyip bellowed, leaping into the lobby like it had spring-loaded feet. For all I knew, that's exactly what it did have. Ellie had cranked the creature's voice up to ear-bleed level, and I could feel the vibrations in the pit of my stomach.

I'd known exactly what was going to come out of the pool and I still got such a shock that I almost fainted.

I could only guess what effect the bunyip was having on everyone else.

I didn't have to wait long to find out.

"Mommy!" Bradley squealed in a voice so loud and high-pitched that dogs in Sydney started barking.

Bradley turned and ran like he was being chased by a flesh-eating zombie bunyip, which, as far as he was concerned, he was. In his blind panic, he ran straight into one of the temporary toilets outside, breaking a pipe and sending a geyser of brown goop all over his perfect hair.

I knew those toilets were going to come into this somewhere.

The rest of the Surf Gorillas weren't doing much better than Bradley. A couple of them flat-out fainted, while Belinda did her best to climb a large potted palm in an attempt to get away.

Operation ROCK was working. Bradley had been publicly humiliated. Revenge was mine!

Except for one small detail.

When I planned this whole thing, the idea was that it would be Bradley—and Bradley alone—in the firing line. Everyone else in Australia's Most Fearless Town would quickly see that the bunyip was a joke, wouldn't they? Ha, ha, ha...?

Khatchadorian, you're such a joker, mate!

Australians liked practical jokes, right? Hadn't Kell told me to lighten up? Rafe Khatchadorian's Great Practical Joke would be the funniest thing ever to happen in Shark's Bay. Right?

Wrong.

Everyone F-R-E-A-K-E-D.

Not just Bradley.

Everyone.

CHAPTER 41

OOPS

Wailing like a police siren, an astronaut leaped off the lobby balcony, landing heavily on a herd of stampeding Elvis dental technicians from the Shark's Bay Dental Clinic.

Nearby, six Salvador Dalis from the Shark's Bay Surrealist Society were trampled underfoot by a bevy of beefy ballerinas from the Bayside Bowling Team. A Viking, a Roman centurion, Frost DeAndrews, and a guy in a giant teddy bear costume were doing their best to hide under the skirts of a howling Queen Victoria, while, to my left, an unconscious Darth Vader was being lifted to safety by a large baby with a beard. Biff Coogan, in his gorilla costume, had scrambled up an ornamental pillar outside the front door, King Kong style, accidentally disturbing a wasps' nest with disastrous results.

A group of leprechauns were fighting to get out of the emergency exit first.

It was pandemonium.

Everywhere there was screaming and running and panic and destruction. Things had gotten waaaay out of hand.

"Kill the bunyip!" I shouted to Ellie. "We have to stop it!"

Ellie wrestled with the remote. "I can't! It's not responding!"

Nico, Sal, Ellie, and I looked helplessly at the bunyip. Little snakes of electricity ran up and down its body, and sparks began shooting from gaps in the creature's skin. It lumbered across the flooded lobby floor, its roar getting louder and louder with every step.

We had created a monster.

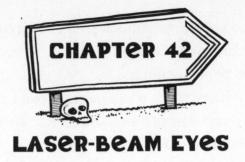

CHAPTER 42

LASER-BEAM EYES

The only real silver lining to this out-of-control Frankenstein scenario was the reaction of Kell Weathers.

The very second Kell glimpsed the bunyip, he dropped his glass, let out a scream almost as high-pitched as Bradley's, and hurled Mom toward the creature before turning on his heel and sprinting for the exit.

Outta my way!

Mom bounced off the bunyip and came to rest on the soaking-wet lobby floor, her face a picture of anger and disgust as she watched

Kell carve a path of yellow-bellied destruction through the screaming crowd.

I wasn't happy that my mom had been treated so badly, but I was kind of glad that she finally got to see Kell for what he really was. If I was going to get in trouble for this (and something told me I was going to get in more trouble for this than for anything I had ever done in my life), then Mom seeing Kell's cowardly streak would make it all worthwhile. She really did deserve better than him.

As if reading my thoughts, she swiveled her head toward me (I swear it rotated 180 degrees), and although it was absolutely impossible for her to have spotted me in the shadows behind the curtains, she zapped a full-strength laser-beam Mom Stare in my direction.

In that split second, I had no doubt at all that she knew.

How do they do that? Moms, I mean. How do they just figure things out so quickly? Is there a special training school? A secret set of mom skills handed to them when you're born?

I sank back into the shadows as Mom got to her feet. This was it. I was about to start a life sentence of being grounded.

It's all in here, Mrs. Khatchadorian. Everything you need to know. Read it and then burn it. We can't allow it to fall into the wrong hands.

But just as I began to trudge toward her to confess that the whole disaster had been my idea, Mom suddenly turned and sighed tiredly, then stalked out of the lobby without a second glance.

I let out a long breath that I didn't know I was holding in. I felt like I'd dodged a bullet, but one thing was for sure—if Mom ever found out for certain that I was the mastermind behind all of this, I was toast. And not the kind with Vegemite.

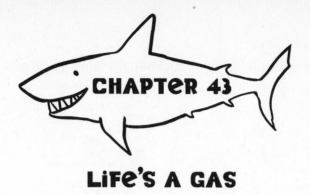

CHAPTER 43

LIFE'S A GAS

Sixty seconds after the bunyip first appeared, there was no one left in the lobby apart from me and the Outsiders. Even the Surf Gorillas who'd fainted had managed to crawl off into the night. Mayor Coogan had slid down his pole at some point and disappeared. There was no sign of Frost DeAndrews or Queen Victoria or my mom, and not a single ballerina, Elvis, pirate, punk, dinosaur, boxer, or bear was to be seen.

Crackling like an out-of-tune radio, the bunyip lurched unsteadily across a floor littered with costume props—false teeth, wigs, eyeglasses, hats, a wooden pirate's leg, a stuffed parrot, the head of a panda. An abandoned camera lay on the floor, the button jammed. It flashed at odd intervals,

making the lobby look as though there were a
lightning storm outside.

"Anything?" I asked Ellie, who was still fiddling
with the remote.

She shook her head. "It's like it's got a mind of
its own."

The bunyip reached the opposite side of the
lobby, hit the wall, then turned toward the open
door. Flames began to lick upward through holes
in the creature's skin.

Sal grabbed a fire extinguisher off the wall. "Well, we can't let it burn the place down."

"Hold on a second, Sal," Ellie said. "It's heading outside."

"There's not too much damage in here," Nico said. "Some water on the floor and a few broken glasses. We could disappear. No one would know it was us."

I had a sudden flashback to Mom looking in my direction when the bunyip appeared. Was I really sure she knew? Or was that just guilt talking? Whatever, Nico's idea was definitely worth considering. Deny everything. Let the bunyip become one of those urban myths.

"Look," Mikey said.

The bunyip had made its way outside and was starting to put some distance

between it and the surf club. Good. Every step it took meant less danger and less of a chance of us being found out. It looked like we were going to be okay.

We followed the bunyip outside and watched it stagger toward the splintered remains of the toilet Bradley had smashed up. It was almost completely on fire now and moved much more slowly. Every so often it made a little electronic beep or squawk, which somehow made it sound weirdly alive. It was like it knew it was dying.

"Maybe the best thing is to let it burn out," Nico said. "Destroy the evidence?"

"Yeah," I said. "That's probably the b—"

Chemistry isn't something I pay much attention to, but as the bunyip crossed the last few feet to the smashed dunnies, one word leaped into my mind like a great big flashing neon sign: *methane*.

"Run!" I yelled.

CHAPTER 44

BOOM!

Methane," Mr. Hernandez had said—yep, the very same Mr. Hernandez whose mustache I yanked on all those pages ago—"is a very combustible gas."

When he was covering science one day, he showed us a film about methane that had been trapped underground and was the cause of a terrible mining disaster. Methane, Mr. Hernandez told us, was produced by rotting vegetation, the underground release of gas from coal mines and rice fields, the digestion systems of cows... and the poop of human

Methane production unit

PARP!

beings. We all laughed at that, which is probably why I remembered it.

A row of portable outdoor toilets was more or less a collecting station for methane, and we had a flaming bunyip on a collision course with one right now.

It was too late for Sal's fire extinguisher.

It was too late to try to fix the remote control.

It was too late to do anything except get out of the way and do it *now*.

As the bunyip finally reached the row of toilets, we turned and ran for our lives. I had no idea how big a methane explosion could be, so I ran about as fast as I have ever run in my life. Every step would take me a little closer to saf—

The universe exploded behind me in a blast of orange light, and I was thrown headfirst through the air.

CHAPTER 45

STARING DEATH RIGHT IN THE FACE

The Grim Reaper's long shadow covered me as he took a couple of steps forward, his heavy scythe sliding across the dry grass. I was glued to the ground. When the robed

figure was no more than a scythe length away, he lifted an arm, and a long white finger pointed directly at me.

"Rafe Khatchadorian," the Grim Reaper said, his voice like dust. "This time you have gone too far. Your time as the Hills Village art representative has come to an end. Your career as an artist is over before it even started. It is time to pay."

My mouth went dry. I tried to say something but I couldn't. Besides, what would I say? "Sorry"? Did the Grim Reaper have a court of appeal?

The Grim Reaper ran a finger along the scythe before pushing back the hood of his robe to reveal a familiar face.

"Mom?" I said.

"No, it's me."

I opened my eyes to see Ellie's face floating above me.

"Can you hear me?"

"You're floating," I said.

"No," Ellie said. "I'm not. You're lying in a ditch."

Ellie had clearly lost her mind, and I was about to tell her exactly that when I realized she was right. I *was* lying in a ditch. I couldn't remember getting there or why I would be there. I didn't even like ditches.

And then it all came back to me, just like that. Bunyip. Fire. Explosion.

Ellie, Nico, Sal, Mikey, and Dingbat came into view. Mikey's eyebrows were singed and Dingbat's head was smoking, but other than that, they seemed fine.

I got to my feet, brushed off the worst of the dirt, and breathed a sigh of relief. This was bad—really bad—but at least I hadn't killed anyone.

"Everyone okay?" I said.

"We're fine," Dingbat replied, "except you did have your butt in my face when we landed."

"You had *your* butt in *my* face," Ellie said with a shudder.

"We're all good," Nico said. "No one's hurt."

We staggered up to the top of the embankment and stood in silence, watching as a great plume of fire and smoke rose from what remained of the toilets and our zombie bunyip.

"Whoa," Dingbat said.

"Whoa" was right. "Whoa" just about covered all the bases.

Lightning zigzagged across the sky, followed closely by a crack of thunder. The storm that had been threatening earlier was about to hit.

I glanced up just as a fat raindrop landed on

my head. Within three seconds, the skies opened and the heaviest rain I've ever seen came down on us. The fire on the remains of the bunyip spat and hissed and then went out like someone had thrown a giant bucket of water over it. In the distance I could see red and blue flashing lights headed our way.

You know how in movies, at moments like this, someone always comes up with a smart line that sums everything up and is kinda cool and tough at the same time?

That doesn't happen in real life.

CHAPTER 46

WHO, ME?

It took Shark's Bay exactly twenty-two minutes to figure out who was behind the Great Surf Club Zombie Bunyip Disaster.

The first hint that no one was going to believe we were innocent came when I arrived back at the Coogans' place. I kinda hoped that I could slink in unnoticed under the cover of darkness. After all, I was soaked to the bone, and all I wanted to do was take a shower, get dry, and get into bed. Instead, everyone was gathered in the living room waiting for me when I opened the door.

All eyes turned to me as I stood there, dripping all over the rug, trying not to look guilty—which, if you've ever tried it, you'll know is a hard look to pull off when you are *innocent*. When you're actually guilty, it's practically impossible.

"Oh," I said. "Hi, everyone."

Bradley, who was wrapped in a blanket, gave me a look of pure hatred.

Ditto Belinda.

Ditto everyone except maybe Mom.

She gave me a look that combined suspicion, shame, anger, fear, and relief. You'd think *that* would be a hard one to manage, but she did it without blinking. Another one of those mom skills, I guess.

"Do you have something to say to us, Rafe?" Biff said.

Barb stood next to him, her arms folded.

Did I? I didn't know. Other than an exploded set of outdoor toilets and a spoiled art exhibition, there was no real harm done, was there? But I needed to give an answer that would deflect all suspicion from me and the Outsiders. Something that would convince everyone that I wasn't involved at all with the bunyip disaster and was just an innocent bystander whose zombie sketches were sadly destroyed.

So, what did I come up with?

I said, "Not really."

Genius.

"You know Bradley was injured?" Mom said.

I looked at Bradley. "What happened?"

"He ran into the woods to get away from whatever that was back there," Barb said, "and got bitten by a possum."

"Doesn't sound too bad," I said.

"That depends where you get bitten," Bradley whimpered. "I might need a rabies shot!"

I tried not to smile, but it was difficult. The idea of a possum giving Bradley a nip in the

privates was just about the
funniest thing I'd ever heard.
And if anyone deserved a rabies
shot, it was Bradley Coogan. I
couldn't stop the smallest smirk
from appearing.

"Any sign of Kell?" I asked
Mom.

She shook her head. Only an
expert on Jules (like me) could tell that she was
about two seconds away from bursting into tears.
My mini smile disappeared like snow on a griddle.
I walked over and gave her a hug.

"I'm sure he'll be fine," I said.

Mom nodded and sniffed. "I hope not," she said,
and we both smiled. I think we were both just
about ready for the night to be over. She told me to
go dry off and get ready for bed.

That wasn't so bad after all. The Coogans were
all suspicious, but it wasn't like anyone had any
proof.

I walked upstairs, dead tired and ready to sleep
for thirty hours.

That's when the mob of zombies arrived.

CHAPTER 47

THERE'S NO REASONING WITH AN ANGRY MOB OF ZOMBIES

Okay, this is where the story started, if you can remember that far back. If not, it might be worth reminding everyone of the situation.

① Zombies, angry mob of. ✓

② Target of angry zombie mob: Rafe Khatchadorian. ✓

③ Pitchforks (yes, really!), flaming torches, chanting. ✓

④ Complete absence of escape plan. ✓

Watching from an upstairs window, I said my prayers and hoped that the mob would stop short of actually killing me, but I couldn't rule it out. The only comfort I had was that the zombie mob wasn't made up of *real* zombies, just an entire town of enraged partygoers who had been frightened half to death by an animatronic bunyip. They still wanted to rip me limb from limb, but at least they probably wouldn't eat me, too.

I don't know how they knew it was me, but maybe they'd just give me a very stern lecture and tell me not to do it again. Maybe when they got real close, they'd see that deep down I was a nice guy and they'd rethink their plans for bloody retribution.

Or, then again, maybe they wouldn't.

And that was just a few of the *nicer* things
they said. Some of the more colorful ones can't be
repeated here. A woman dressed as Tinker Bell,
whom I recognized as the local librarian, was
swearing so much I thought her head was going to
explode.

"Oh, boy," Leo muttered. "This is worse than I thought."

"Gee, is that supposed to cheer me up?" I turned around, but Leo had vanished. Even my imaginary brother had chickened out.

I leaned closer to the window and saw Biff Coogan below me, standing outside the front door, arguing with the ringleaders. I couldn't hear much of what Biff was saying, but I think he was pointing out that, while I probably deserved anything they were suggesting as punishment, he, Biffly Algernon Coogan, mayor of Shark's Bay, could not stand by and watch his American guest being torn limb from limb.

"Think of the publicity!" Biff reasoned. "And the mess! The police will want to know what happened to him."

"No, we won't!" a man dressed as a punk rocker said. "I'm Sergeant Justin Carter Hatfield, and most of the department is already here."

"And the fire department," someone else shouted.

"Everyone's here, Biff!" Sergeant Hatfield said. "So let us at the little blot, and we'll see he gets what's coming!"

Biff was clearly jolted by the unexpected appearance of the Shark's Bay Police Department, but he did a good job of not letting it show. He crossed his arms and jutted out his chin defiantly. "Now, that might be the case, Justin, but it's still no way for a town to b—"

"There he is!" Bradley squealed like a pig with a trench full of slops.

Everyone looked up at me, and the effect was like dropping a match on a gasoline-soaked bonfire. A great roar rose from the mob, and all the pitchforks and flaming torches were lifted into the air. The zombies pushed Biff aside like he was made of straw and swarmed toward the door.

I was doomed.

CHAPTER 48

MiGHTY MOM

Stop right there!"

A voice crackled through the night. It was like an atomic bomb going off, and it stopped the mob dead in its tracks. It was a voice that demanded to be obeyed. It was the ultimate voice of authority.

It was the voice of Mom the All-Powerful.

I ran out of my room, leaned over the rail of the stairway, and looked down at the hallway below.

Mom, wearing her superhero costume and a steely expression, faced down the mob. She stood toe to toe with Sergeant Hatfield, her hands on her hips.

"No one move a muscle," Mom snarled. She jabbed the cop in the chest with a finger. "If anyone so much as *touches* my kid, they'll have *me* to deal with. Understand?"

Now, I'm not a kid who cries much, but I have to admit my eyes welled up a little seeing my mom like that. There wasn't a tiger on earth who would have protected her cub with more determination or sharper claws. If Hatfield and the rest of the zombie mob knew what was good for them, they'd quit now.

"He's made a fool of us all!" Hatfield barked. "He's got to pay!"

Behind him, the mob muttered agreement.

"He's made a fool of Shark's Bay!" a voice yelled from the back.

"I hate him!" Bradley declared.

"He puked on me!" Belinda shouted.

A few of the mob did double takes, as if they hadn't heard right. *Not only is this guy a slimy bunyip releaser,* I could hear them thinking, *he's also a low-life puker?*

"And these pitchforks cost money!" someone else piped up.

Mom stepped forward. "First of all, there's no proof that Rafe was involved in *anything.*"

I gulped. Mom was on thin ice here. *I* was on thin ice.

CRACK!

One false move and the mob would push her aside and start handing out some homemade justice. But Mom wasn't finished, not by a long shot.

"And second of all," she said, raising her voice, "if he *was* involved, then he *has* made a fool of you all." Mom's voice got sharper, something I didn't believe possible until I heard it for myself. It had an edge to it that could have sharpened a samurai sword. "And I imagine the rest of Australia would be very interested to see exactly how Australia's Most Fearless Town ran away from a rubber *toy*."

I could almost see everyone's brains working as they processed the information. Mom was right. If this got out, Shark's Bay would become a laughingstock.

Ha! Ha! Hahaha!

Justin Carter Hatfield narrowed his eyes. "Are you threatening us?"

"That's rich," Mom said, "coming from a police officer holding a pitchfork and standing at the head of an angry mob coming to hunt down my kid."

She had a point.

"But, yes, since you mention it," she continued, "it *is* a threat. Now get off my property!"

Technically, it was Biff and Barb Coogan's property, but we all knew what she meant.

"No one will believe you bunch of blow-ins!" Hatfield said. "Where's your proof?"

"Right here." Ellie stepped forward out of the crowd and held up her phone.

Her finger hovered over the screen. "If I press this button, the evidence will be uploaded to the internet. Everyone will see how you all ran away from my silly puppet. And how *you* knocked over an old granny in your rush for the door, Sergeant Hatfield. It's pretty shocking, if you ask me. It might even go viral."

"How did you find that?" Sergeant Hatfield asked incredulously.

Ellie smiled. "I filmed the whole thing."

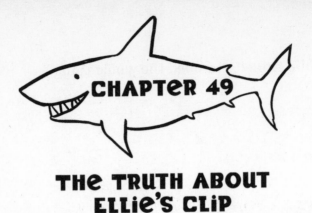

CHAPTER 49

THE TRUTH ABOUT ELLIE'S CLIP

We planted cameras around the surf club," Ellie said smugly to the crowd. "I just spent the last hour editing, and now the clip is waiting to be uploaded to my video channel. I just need to press one little button." She paused dramatically and eyeballed the mob.

Ellie looked at Hatfield, who, it seemed, had assumed the role of leader of the (almost) zombie mob.

"So what you have to ask yourself is: 'Do I feel lucky?' Well, do ya, punk?"

That's a line from a movie, in case you didn't know.

It turned out he wasn't feeling very lucky after all.

And neither was the rest of the zombie mob. They lowered their pitchforks and flaming torches. Faced with a choice between getting their revenge on me (assuming they could get past the Mom of Steel) and facing global humiliation versus just backing down, the mob chose to back down. One by one they began to drift off into the rain-swept darkness.

Ellie stepped through the front door and shook the water from her dark hair.

"Were you really going to upload the clip?" I whispered.

Ellie lowered her phone and smiled. "What clip?"

CHAPTER 50

KANGAROOS SUCK

If you don't mind, I'll skip over the rest of my time in Shark's Bay as quickly as possible.

Long story short, it wasn't pleasant.

Mom postponed any punishment over my possible involvement in the Great Surf Club Zombie Bunyip Disaster until we were home.

The Coogans treated us well enough for the remainder of our stay—by which I mean they treated us like we were basically radioactive. The weather may have been hot outside, but the temperature at 22 Sunspot Crescent was arctic. It was official: the cultural exchange experiment between Hills Village and Shark's Bay had been a total disaster.

I didn't even see Bradley or Belinda again

before we left, which was just fine by me. I could happily spend the rest of my life never seeing either of the twins ever again, and they must have felt exactly the same. In that way, and that way alone, we had something in common.

After having time to think about it, I decided that it had been worth it. No one had been badly injured (unless you counted Bradley having his privates nibbled by a possum), no real damage had been done (other than one exploded row of temporary toilets), and I had gotten my revenge for being publicly humiliated (three times!). Not to mention, the Surf Gorillas finally got punished for wrecking *Revenge of the Teenage Zombie Bunyip from Mars.*

All in all, I reflected, they deserved what they'd gotten.

And as for Ellie and the Outsiders, Ellie and I talked until late that night. I won't tell you what we said or how we left it. That's just for me and Ellie. Meeting her and the Outsiders had been the highlight of my trip. I wouldn't forget them or regret a single thing about coming to Australia.

Except not seeing a kangaroo. I hadn't seen a single one of those overgrown hopping rats.

Now, *that* sucked.

CHAPTER 51

ATTACK OF THE FIFTY-FOOT CONSCIENCE MONSTER

I'm sorry about Kell," I said to Mom. "I mean, I did think he was a total jerk and all, but I know you liked him. I shouldn't have been so happy when he...you know..."

"When he threw me in the way of the bunyip and ran for his life, screaming like a three-year-old who saw the boogeyman?" Mom said.

"Maybe that's what geologists are like," I offered.

"I don't think so, Rafe. I'm sure there are plenty of brave geologists out there. Just not Kell."

I hate Australian geologists!

"Anyway," I said, "you liked him and I'm sorry he did what he did."

We were 38,000 feet above the Pacific Ocean, about halfway back to Hills Village.

Mom shrugged. "I thought I liked him, but he turned out to be someone different from who I thought he was. I suppose I can thank you for that. But I'm fine, honestly, Rafe. Just fine."

Mom put her headphones back on and started watching a movie. I noticed that none of her lucky charms were visible and that she seemed pretty calm for someone terrified of flying. I guess that after everything that had gone on in Shark's Bay, an airplane flight didn't seem like such a big deal anymore.

I sat back in my seat and listened to the sound of the engines.

I was home free. So why didn't I feel better?

The answer came to me somewhere over Hawaii. There was the obvious stuff like missing Ellie and the rest of the guys, but that wasn't it. No, what was bugging me was that we—me and the Outsiders—had done something *great,* something really cool and challenging and awesome and creative, and no one outside Shark's Bay would ever know.

And we never got to make our film.

CHAPTER 52

I WAS A TEENAGE OUTSIDER (AND I LIKED IT)

I did get grounded when we got home. But that was fair. I deserved it. I *did* ruin the trip, after all.

I've been talking to Ellie online. She mentioned she might make a trip to Hills Village before too long. "And I'm working on something cool. Keep your eye on your mailbox, okay?" she added.

I tried to get her to say more, but she wouldn't. Nothing much had changed for her in Shark's Bay.

"We were always the Outsiders," she said. "That's the way I like it."

That's a good way of looking at things. I'm kind of an outsider in Hills Village. The thing is, before I met Ellie and the rest of the Outsiders, I always saw that as a negative. Maybe I've been looking at things the wrong way. Instead of trying to fit in with everyone else, maybe I'd be better off *not* fitting in and liking it.

I've started to get more interested in filmmaking, too. I even started working on some storyboards for my own movie. A horror movie, of course.

Best of all, I've realized that I learned something important on the trip. It was something my mom said in between telling me how grounded I was. She said that bravery comes in many forms and she thought I was brave for producing art.

"At least you're trying," she said. "You might be

scared of sharks and snakes and imaginary drop bears, but who isn't?"

She stopped short of actually saying she approved of me letting an animatronic zombie bunyip loose on Shark's Bay, but let's be honest— *that* was never going to happen.

Being back home felt good. On the upside, it was great to see Grandma Dotty and Junior and Flip. On the downside, I was back under the same roof as Georgia.

There was one especially great thing about being back in Hills Village. As my feet slid between the sheets, I was pretty sure that there wouldn't be any snakes.

TOTAL CONTENTMENT

CHAPTER 53

AN ARTIST LIKE KHATCHADORIAN

Wait! I forgot to mention the best part! Probably the greatest thing to come out of the whole trip (apart from meeting Ellie).

Four weeks after arriving back, I got a weird package marked with Australian stamps in the mail.

Inside it was a rolled-up magazine and a note from Ellie. All it said was: *Pages 32–34.*

I carefully unrolled the magazine. It was something called the *Great Australian Art Monthly*—a big, thick, glossy thing full of articles about famous

Australian artists and artists who were visiting Australia from all over the world.

I flicked to page 32 and almost passed out.

It was a picture of the bunyip ripping through the lobby of the Shark's Bay Surf Club. It had been taken on a phone camera and was a little fuzzy, but it still looked awesome. The bunyip's mouth was open and sparks were shooting out. People were screaming and running in the background. The headline read ZOMBIE MOVIE ART TRIUMPH AT SHARK'S BAY, and it was written by Frost DeAndrews.

"I thought I had been fooled," DeAndrews wrote, "when the *Zombie Movie* exhibition I had been invited to at sleepy little Shark's Bay

turned out to be nothing more than a collection of passable sketches by visiting young American artist Rafe Khatchadorian.

"But I was deeply mistaken. In one of the most scintillating and brave performance art productions I have seen in recent years, Khatchadorian and his art group, the Outsiders, ran us right through the A–Z of contemporary performance art and treated us to a totally immersive experience not seen since the days of Wilhelm Van Purpleschpittel and the neocolonial burble movement...."

The rest of the article was illustrated with more photos of the whole event and had interviews with Ellie and the guys, and a lot of art speak I didn't understand. Even Mayor Coogan got in on the act.

"Rafe insisted on keeping everything top secret," he said. "We're very proud of Shark's Bay's association with an artist like Khatchadorian."

An artist like Khatchadorian.

It had a ring to it. I liked it.

"Mom!" I shouted, leaping off my bed. "You gotta see this!"

VICTOR COMES FROM A BIG FAMILY OF SUPERVILLAINS, BUT HE JUST WANTS TO BE A NICE, NORMAL KID. HIS PARENTS WONDER... WHERE DID THEY GO WRONG?

Check out this sneak preview of

HOW TO BE A SUPERVILLAIN

Available May 2017!

We weren't halfway down the block before the Smear started my supervillain education. "Pay attention, kid. There's a lot to learn."

I reached into my backpack and pulled out a notebook and pen.

"What are you doing?" said the Smear.

"Taking notes."

The Smear grabbed my notebook and threw it out the window. "First lesson: supervillains NEVER take notes!"

"How will I remember anything?" I asked.

"You pay attention! With a fierce, burning passion to do evil."

"We'll work on it," said the Smear. "First, let's talk stains."

He started by describing various custom smear-stains and their effect on superheroes.

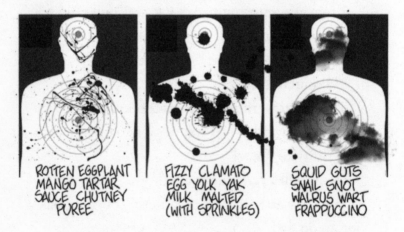

"Can you pick up walrus warts at Costco?" I wondered out loud.

"A little less talking and a little more listening," he said.

Then he turned to his patented stain delivery systems, including, but not limited to, stain blasters...

I said, "What about your eyes? Can you spray stains with your eyes?"

"No," he said. "That would be weird. And really unsanitary."

Then he described a stain bomber.

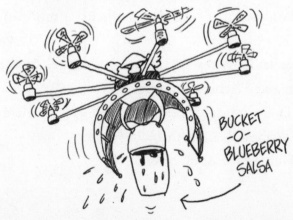

BUCKET
-O-
BLUEBERRY
SALSA

"Yum. I'll have some blueberry salsa," I said.

He shook his head. "No. We don't eat the weapons."

"Got it," I said.

Next up was the Stainmixer...

BAD QUESO DIP

"Wouldn't a flying dump truck be more efficient?" I asked.

He said, "Where's your sense of style? Anyone can make a flying dump truck."

Finally, he described a platoon of specialized, highly trained, stain-throwing mice.

"Trained mice?" I asked.

The Smear gestured to the backseat.

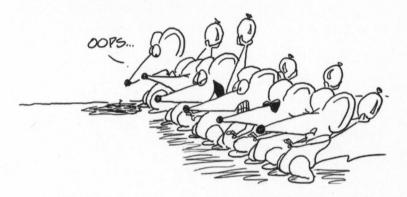

OOPS...

I turned back around and stared at the road ahead. "This is going to get strange, isn't it?"
The Smear chuckled. "You have no idea."

Read more in

HOW TO BE A SUPERVILLAIN

Available May 2017!

Sticks and stones
may break your bones,
but mean names
last forever!

GET A SNEAK PEEK AT

Pottymouth
and
Stoopid

COMING JUNE 2017!

The Blame Game

When you're Pottymouth and Stoopid, you get blamed for all sorts of stuff you didn't actually do.

Remember that disgusting lunch in the cafeteria?

The mystery meat in the mushy sauce on a bed of rice that might've been moving? The one everybody called "When You Find Out What It Is, Don't Tell Me"?

Well, somehow, that was our fault.

"Stoopid gave them

the recipe," went the rumor. "And Pottymouth told them to pour schnizzleflick all over it."

When the basketball team lost its first game, everybody blamed Michael.

"Pottymouth called the other team fluffer-knuckles. That's why we lost. He fired up the enemy with his pottymouthing!"

Not true, of course, but the truth seldom has anything to do with a good Pottymouth or Stoopid story.

For instance, did you know that I'm the one who opened the hamster cage in the fifth-grade classroom and set Scruffy free? Yeah, I didn't know it either. From what I heard, I saw the word *ham* on the cage. I thought there was a sandwich inside and I was hungry.

Then there was that disastrous field trip to the natural history museum. The trip when the whole *Tyrannosaurus rex* skeleton in the lobby toppled to the ground. They say I yanked out an anklebone so I could take it home to my dog.

I don't even have a dog, I told anybody who'd listen. Which would be nobody.

When Anna started hanging out with us, she got blamed for stuff too.

The power outage during the big vampire battle scene in the movie everybody was watching during study hall?

"Anna Britannica pulled the plug on the extension cord," proclaimed Kaya Kennecky. "She thought it was a bright orange Twizzler and tried to eat it."

And so it went. Day after day.

Pottymouth did this. Stoopid did that. Anna Britannica did everything else.

I realized that Michael and I had been Pottymouth and Stoopid for so long, most of the kids at school didn't know our real names.

That was okay, I guess.

Because we didn't want to know their names either.

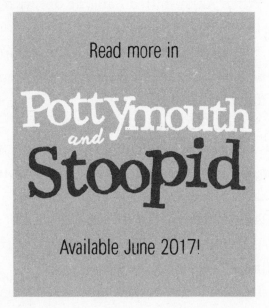

Read more in

Pottymouth
and
Stoopid

Available June 2017!

ABOUT THE AUTHORS

JAMES PATTERSON received the Literarian Award for Outstanding Service to the American Literary Community at the 2015 National Book Awards. He holds the Guinness World Record for the most #1 *New York Times* bestsellers, including *Middle School, I Funny,* and *Jacky Ha-Ha,* and his books have sold more than 350 million copies worldwide. A tireless champion of the power of books and reading, Patterson created a children's book imprint, JIMMY Patterson, whose mission is simple: "We want every kid who finishes a JIMMY Book to say, 'PLEASE GIVE ME ANOTHER BOOK.'" He has donated more than one million books to students and soldiers, and funds over four hundred Teacher Education Scholarships at twenty-four colleges and universities. He has also donated millions to independent bookstores and school libraries. Patterson invests proceeds from the sales of JIMMY Patterson Books in pro-reading initiatives.

MARTIN CHATTERTON was born in Liverpool, England, and has been successfully writing and illustrating books for almost thirty years. He has written dozens of children's books and illustrated many more for other writers, including several British Children's Laureates. His work has been published in fourteen languages and has won and been short-listed in numerous awards in the UK, US, and Australia. In addition to writing for children, Chatterton writes crime fiction (as Ed Chatterton), continues to work as a graphic designer, and is currently working on his PhD. Having lived in the US, Chatterton now divides his time between Australia and the UK.

DANieL GRiFFO was always drawn toward creating and drawing images. In his teens, he became a self-taught comic illustrator and worked for both Argentinean and Italian publishers. As a freelance illustrator, Griffo has worked for many large companies, including Image Comics, Warner, and Scholastic. He currently resides in Argentina with his wife and children.